SIGN OF THE HAWK

**Center Point
Large Print**

**This Large Print Book carries the
Seal of Approval of N.A.V.H.**

SIGN OF THE HAWK
A Western Duo

MAX BRAND

A Circle Ⓥ Western

CENTER POINT PUBLISHING
THORNDIKE, MAINE

This Circle V Western is published by
Center Point Large Print in the year 2008
in cooperation with Golden West Literary Agency.

Copyright © 2008 by Golden West Literary Agency.

The text of this Large Print edition is unabridged. In other
aspects, this book may vary from the original edition.
Printed in the United States of America.
Set in 16-point Times New Roman type.

ISBN: 978-1-60285-162-7

Cataloging-in-Publication data is available from the Library of Congress.

Acknowledgments

"The Singular Horseman" by Max Brand first appeared in *Collier's* (6/27/36). Copyright © 1936 by Crowell Collier Publishing Company. Copyright © renewed 1964 by the Estate of Frederick Faust. Copyright © 2008 by Golden West Literary Agency for restored material.

"Sign of the Hawk" first appeared under the title "The Mask of Ching Wo", a six-part serial by Max Brand in *Railroad Man's Magazine* (8/30-1/31). Copyright © 1930 by the Frank A. Munsey Company. Copyright © renewed 1958 by Dorothy Faust. Copyright © 2008 by Golden West Literary Agency for restored material.

TABLE OF CONTENTS

The Singular Horseman

By 1936, Frederick Faust had abandoned what had been his primary story market, Street & Smith's *Western Story Magazine*, due to decreases in the rate he was paid per word. While his stories still appeared in a number of pulps—*Argosy* and *Detective Fiction Weekly*—his market was expanding to the slicks, *Cosmopolitan, McCall's Magazine, The Saturday Evening Post*, and *Collier's*. It was in *Collier's* that "The Singular Horseman" appeared in the June 27, 1936 issue, one of four stories of his to appear in that magazine that year. This is its first appearance in book form.

There is a type of horse that should be known as Roman-Nosed Fool or Staring Jackass. It may possess every quality of strength and conformation; it may jump like a rabbit and run like a deer all day long, but it has barely enough brains to tell oats from hay and generally gallops with an open mouth and glaring idiocy in the eyes. Since youth, my habit has been to keep one of these creatures in my string of hunters, not because I believe in self-martyrdom but in order to strengthen my grip, sensitize my touch, and develop the cold patience that can be such a treasure to every man who follows the hounds.

However, I never expected to find among men a counterpart of these witless brutes, far less that it should be a blood relation. If the madness of Terence Barnes was only temporary, it was yet extremely real, and I still think with bewilderment of the time when young Terry took the bit between his teeth and bolted downhill. The shock was greater to me because, when I visited his father in California, I found Terry a promising youth with a conservative seat and an intelligent pair of hands. In polo he was a little too apt to play the ball, instead of the man, but on the whole I considered that he was being well formed to fit into the right tradition.

Terry was still in California, so far as I knew, when I came in from an hour's session with Sedgewick, my Roman-nosed idiot of the season, and found Terence

11

Barnes in the library, his forehead resting on a clenched fist.

"Well, Terry, what are you doing here?" I asked.

"She's your neighbor," he said. He came to me hurriedly and added: "I've got to meet her! Will you ask them over? Or will you take me there?"

Manners, I thank God, still are prized in all the branches of my family, and I was sufficiently shocked by this abrupt greeting. He was not even aware that my hand was held out to him. I used it to pick up a cigarette. In the meantime, I surveyed him and saw that his face was pale, his eyes round and staring.

"Who is she?" I asked.

"She's lovely," answered Terry.

Some Scotch and soda came in. I was glad to interrupt this headless conversation by pouring drinks because I was being reminded more and more forcibly of Sedgewick by the blank emotion of Terence Barnes. If he were touched in the brain, what a pity, what a waste, for he had that true build of the rider, light and strong, which God has granted to so many of the Barneses and Whitlocks.

In the meantime, he was striding rapidly up and down the room with the aspiring step that Shakespeare notes about Diomedes and which I have observed in all natural athletes.

"I'll have mine straight," said Terry.

"A rider never should drink straight liquor before dinner," I told him. "A true horseman. . . ."

"Damn horsemen!" said Terry.

It was a warm, bright day with the windows open to the beauty of it, but now a slight chill worked through my blood. Clearly he had been touched in the brain.

He went on: "That's the trouble! Isn't it true, sir? This whole countryside is simply swarming with able horsemen."

Without passion, as one would deal with a Sedgewick, using always a delicate touch, I answered: "It is true that we manage a fairly good hunt."

"And you're the M.F.H., Mister Whitlock, aren't you?" he asked.

I admitted that I was a master of fox hounds.

He poured his whiskey down his throat at a gulp. Then he went on: "You can tell me the truth. Isn't your hunt packed with fine six-footers, all bred right, all schooled properly, all of them ready to jump hell and high water for the sake of Elena Casimir-Jones?"

I smiled.

"My dear Terry," I said, "naturally the boys pay attention to a pretty child like Elena."

"Pretty?" cried Terence, staring at me. "Child? Pretty . . . ? She's divine!"

"Really? When did you meet her?"

"I haven't met her. She's always surrounded by a herd of fellows . . . all horsemen, too. I could tell it by the straightness of their backs and the slight blear of their eyes."

"That's true," I said. "There is usually a crowd around Elena. However, it might be arranged. . . ."

"Arrange it now, sir, will you?" he begged. "Let me

see her, please! And if she's tired of foxhunters. . . ."

Now that I have aftersight to help me, it is plain that I should have paused at this moment to make a closer inquiry as to what was in his mind. The last words should have warned me. "*If she's tired of fox-hunters . . .* " had an important significance, but, knowing the bloodlines of the Barneses and Whit-locks, how could I have dreamed of what was to come? As easily imagine a thoroughbred that will eat apples or refuse to jump.

Without the least hesitation, I went to the telephone and rang Barry Casimir-Jones.

"I'm coming over for dinner if it's convenient," I said.

"Good," said Barry. "Some of the lads will be here with Elena. You and I can have a quiet evening together. I have found a great old fine champagne, a Monnet."

"Monnet?" I said.

"Monnet!" said Barry.

Then I remembered to add: "Young cousin of mine. . . . I'm bringing him along."

When I turned from the telephone, Terence demanded: "Is it all right, sir? Is it all right for me to go?"

"If you're not a silly young ass, of course it's all right," I told him. "Now sit down and tell me about your people in California. How is that bay mare by Scepter coming on?"

"I'll tell you all the news when there's a chance,"

14

said Terry, wringing my hand in the most grateful way. "But now I have to work. I have to work like the devil till dinnertime. . . . Will somebody show me my room . . . ? I'm not crowding you, Judge Whitlock, am I . . . ? Shall I wear a white tie or a dinner jacket?"

It was *impossible* to answer him, so I did not try. I rang for the butler and told him to take Terry to the southwest room, then I went back to my Scotch and soda, and an uneasy thought of the similarity that, somehow, existed between Sedgewick and my unhappy young relation—that moon-struck blankness—disturbed me.

A good part of my concern left me when he came down in tails to go with me to the Casimir-Jones place, for, like all his kin, he looked the blood that was in him, good, keen eyes and a chin pushed up in the air a bit to look over the next jump. For my part, I rarely can look at a Whitlock or a Barnes without thinking of a sharp winter morning and the cry of the running pack.

On the way over, he said: "Has she been engaged often?"

"Why, I don't know," I answered. "I think there was something about Stewart Tillinghast, and now there's Dyke Vincent, I believe. Old playmates, you know."

"It's damned indecent," said Terry.

"What's indecent?" I asked.

"The way men take advantage of a young girl," said Terry.

I had to agree with him. I still was talking about the

free manners of the younger vintage when we reached the big quiet dignity of the Casimir-Jones house. People today have forgotten how to build places where there is room for everything.

As we went up to the door, Terence said: "If I seem a little different, tonight, I hope you won't make any remarks to the others, sir."

If the lad realized that he was in a jitter, of course, it was best not to use a curb on him. I told him so.

"No matter what I say, you won't bring me up short?" he asked.

"Certainly not," I said.

He was so solemn about it that he wanted to shake hands on the bargain, and, of course, I was willing, although at this point a damaging premonition for the first time began to trouble me, just as I can tell the coming of a norther by the ache in my broken shoulder.

We went in among a rattle of young voices. There were a dozen or more youths of the neighborhood—two or three girls and the rest were boys of the hunt. I introduced Terry, and then had an old-fashioned in a corner of the room with Barry Casimir-Jones. Elena had not come down.

"Trim-looking fellow, young Barnes," said Barry. "You could mount him on a lightweight, in a pinch, I suppose. What a lot of money that saves."

He looked down, sadly. In fact, Barry has let his middle section get a little out of hand; he had granted a bit too much to the coming of years and dignity.

Then Elena came in, and I saw poor Terry white and straight as a spy before a firing squad. I was between a smile and pity, although at that very moment the fellow was gathering himself for the frightfulness that was about to come. About that, of course, I could know nothing. All that I noticed before we went into dinner was that, when Terry took her hand, he bowed over it after a fashion that I had to learn and unlearn while I was still a boy.

Elena slanted a questioning glance at me as we poured into the dining room to sit around the endless table of the Casimir-Joneses. Terry, as the stranger, was given the place at Elena's right hand. He looked a bit pale and strained, I thought, but just then young Harry Bell began to ask my advice about a colt he wanted to buy and I lost track of Terry for a moment while I pointed out that the colt was full of Carry Over blood, and the Carry Over strain notoriously cannot stay. It was in the midst of this talk—and the fish—that a sudden silence spread from Elena's end of the table, and out of the quiet I distinctly heard Terence Barnes state: "The fact is that I know nothing about horses, except that Tu Fu taught me to be fond of them."

I stared at him and found him wearing a gentle, idiotic smile such as I never before had seen on the face of a Barnes or a Whitlock.

"Too few what?" asked big Dyke Vincent.

"I mean Tu Fu, the great Chinese poet," said Terry.

At that moment I recalled several things: Terry's

expressed determination to make himself "different" from the horsy crowd who surrounded Elena; his afternoon of study in his room; above all the strangely serious bargain that he had driven with me at the door of the Casimir-Jones house. My premonition of trouble turned into a horrible certainty as I saw exactly the face that the disgrace would wear.

"I never heard that the fat-faced Chinamen had poets," said Dyke Vincent.

"Have you never?" answered the gentle voice of Terry. "Well, after all, Tu Fu died over a thousand years ago. That is to say, if great poets ever die. Do you think they do?"

He had turned to Elena.

She grew a little warm in the face and said: "Well. . . ."

By this time eyes were beginning to turn to me with covert questioning, but I occupied myself in chasing a bit of sole with my fork and wishing Terence Barnes at the devil's gate.

He was saying: "I've always liked to think that they go on . . . the poets. Their thoughts, at least. You know how one is overtaken, now and then, in the quiet times when one is alone? Thoughts that are not one's own. . . ."

He made a gesture at space.

Barry Casimir-Jones said: "Well, well."

Stewart Tillinghast pressed his lips together, but the grin spilled out of the corners of his mouth.

I remembered that I was a Whitlock; I tried to recall that Terry was a Barnes.

Then Elena lifted her head and said to the length of the table: "I think that's charming. I really think it's a lovely thought."

"Do you?" asked Dyke Vincent.

"Yes, I do," she said. "I'd like to know more about Tu Fu. And what did he say about horses? You haven't had much to do with them?"

"I never learned to ride," said Terence Barnes. He had the effrontery to meet my eye and pass it over. The whole table was struck to a silence. "But I know they're beautiful," went on Terry. "Tu Fu rings out like a bell when he sings about them."

I grabbed my glass of white wine because my throat was closing like a fist. It was a delicious Montrachet, properly iced, and after a good deep swallow of it I could breathe again.

"How does Tu Fu speak about horses?" asked Elena. "What does he say of them?"

"I remember that he speaks about the Tartar horses and their ears as sharp as split bamboo," said Terence Barnes. "That's rather good. Don't you think so, Mister Vincent?"

Dyke Vincent looked straight back at him. "No, I *don't* think so," he said.

"But wait a minute, Dyke," said Elena. "It's quite delightful. You know just how sharp and thin the ear of a thoroughbred can be."

"There are a lot of things too thin for me," said Dyke.

Tillinghast broke in: "I don't know much about split

bamboo. But did they really have horses in China?"

"Heavens, Stew! That's where they originated, isn't it?" asked Elena.

She leaned a little toward Terry as though her smile and her voice were not enough to draw him out.

"At least," said Terry, "Tu Fu was very fond of them. He wrote a number of long *hsing* and *ko* about the celebrated horses of the sons of heaven."

Tillinghast kept from talk. He was darkly watchful, but Dyke Vincent went on.

"I knew about Chinese printing and Chinese gunpowder," he said. "But I never heard about their horses. Did they really go?"

"You know," said Terry, "they went so well that Mu Wang drove to the western paradise with a team of eight of the dragon's blood."

"Dragon's blood by what?" said Dyke.

"Dyke, are you going to be simply an idiot?" asked Elena. "Dragon's blood . . . in China it means the best . . . everything imperial and top-hole in China they call dragon's blood. You know."

"No, I didn't know," said Dyke. "Funny lot of thugs, aren't they? The chinks . . . I mean to say. What did they feed their horses? Split bamboo or something?"

"Yao Niao used to be fed by the emperor himself," said Terry. "Rice out of a golden bowl."

"Rice! Damned bad for the poor horse," said Dyke. "What you say, Uncle Barry, about rice for a horse?" he called down the table. "Rice, Jack!" he said to me.

"Rice, eh?" laughed Barry.

"Ha!" I said, because there seemed nothing else to say.

Elena broke out: "Can't you see that it's poetry?"

"May be poetry," said Barry, "but it's damned poor horse feed, I'll assure you."

"I wish you'd recite them something splendid about horses from Tu Fu this minute!" exclaimed Elena.

"Certainly," said Terence.

He threw back his head a little and looked at the ceiling for a moment while Elena dreamed over him with half-shut eyes. I closed mine entirely. She kept nodding a little and smiling like a mother waiting for her baby son to astonish the world by taking a first step. The dreamy face of Terry began to brighten and lighten pretty soon. Then he chanted, singing out the words in a soft drawl:

Of the swift horses,
the wild horses in the stables of the son of heaven,
Help me to sing,
of the horses who gallop ten thousand li,
Ten thousand li *from the furnace of dawn*
until their hoofs
Are cooled in the pool of night,
in the meadows of darkness.

"How far is a *li?*" said Barry.

"A quarter of a mile," said Terry.

"Those horses used to gallop ten thousand *li* in a day, did they?" said Barry.

"In the poem," said Elena.

"I'm not complaining," said her father.

"You know," explained Elena, "the essence of poetry is exaggeration."

Terry began to intone again, quietly—you might say after the modest manner of the fellow to whom you can listen or not, as you please.

"Purple eyes," he droned, "set in a square frame!

How beautiful!
Gray and black his body, like new silver and old,
His two trembling ears are yellow. . . ."

"Yellow ears?" said Barry. "On a gray horse?"

"The Chinese had the most exquisite sense of color!" cried Elena.

The table hummed with low laughing. Dyke tried to keep from laughing, but somehow couldn't hold in. He bellowed loudly.

Terry was not offended. "Oh, is it funny?" he said, and smiled in a pitiful sort of way, as though he wanted to see the joke.

But Elena's glance ruled a bright line across the table and poured fire upon Dyke Vincent.

"Do you happen to know, Dyke," she said, "that Tu Fu is the greatest poet in China?"

"Is he . . . of China?" said Dyke. "Sorry, Elena. Awfully sorry, Barnes."

"Not at all," said Terry. "Of course one doesn't get the full effect in translations. They used to chant them . . . like this. . . ."

A stallion squealed just then from the stables and we heard a pounding against a wooden wall like a dozen drummers breaking their big bass drums. Barry Casimir-Jones pushed back his chair.

"There goes Starboard again!" he exclaimed. He pulled his chair up to the table again and sighed. "Well, no good of me going out to see him. The villain! He's got to wear his tantrums out."

"I hope he's not killing one of the grooms," said Elena darkly. "He's going to do a murder one of these days."

"But murder?" said Terry.

Barry rolled his eyes toward me, but I could not speak; I could hardly swallow.

"It's the whole trouble," said Elena. "You people just breed horses for speed, speed, speed . . . just running machines to rip across country and crash themselves and kill their masters . . . I think Mister Barnes is right. A lot of horses are better left to poetry."

"Come, come," said Barry.

"Frightful," said Terry, opening his eyes again.

"But I mean to say, Elena," said Barry, "how many riders are killed, actually?"

"Take in this very last year!" exclaimed Elena. "Tommy Wayland *worse* than dead . . . and Margaret Vane. . . ."

A good bit of stage thunder came out of the stables once more.

"Frightful," breathed Terry. "Shouldn't he be destroyed?"

"He should," said Elena, "except that his bloodlines . . . well, you wouldn't understand, but. . . ."

"He's never been ridden in a race," said Casimir-Jones sadly. "He bolts, or runs the wrong way, or jumps a fence . . . he can't be trained . . . and God knows that it's a peril even to keep him in a box stall."

"Have you tried apples?" asked Terry.

"What?" exclaimed Barry.

"I mean," said Terry, "have you tried to gentle him with apples and things?"

"I have tried things," Casimir-Jones said when he was able to speak, "but I have not tried apples."

The wretched dinner ended at last, and I had to face Casimir-Jones in a corner of the library.

He said: "Ah . . . your young cousin is an interesting chap . . . very unusual."

"*Ha* . . . ," I said, because for the second time that evening I could say nothing else.

"Well," said Barry, "in the most unexpected places. . . . However, let's try this Monnet."

We tried it, but I had almost lost my sense of taste. At the earliest decent moment I rounded up Terry and told him that we had to go home. His eyes begged me silently, like the look of a hunting dog when it sees the master done up in shooting togs, but I was happy to pretend not to understand.

The good night between him and Elena was a thing to remember. She wanted him to come again, any time, and read Tu Fu to her. They had progressed to first names.

"If you'll come over tomorrow morning," said Elena, "I'll teach you to ride. You know . . . on a *very* gentle horse."

On the way home I wished to heaven that we could talk freely but we were in an infernal all-weather body with nothing between us and the chauffeur. Instead of speaking my thoughts, I was forced to keep on thinking, and all that I could envision was that inevitable future meeting with Casimir-Jones. No explanation would be possible. How could Barry believe that I had allowed the young scoundrel to tie my hands with a promise before he began his crooked operations?

At last we were standing in the hall of my house, but when I saw the face of Terry, my teeth shut over the words that were rising. I could only say: "At least you made yourself . . . different."

"Yes, sir," said Terry, and swallowed. The act seemed to give him pain, I am glad to say.

"Where did you run on this damned Tu Fu?" I asked.

"In a newspaper review," said Terry. "It seemed so cock-eyed that I bought a copy of the book. I wanted to see what people *will* read."

"Where did you get that stuff about dead poets not dying?" I demanded.

"It was all in the review, sir," he said.

"What do you expect to get out of this?" I asked.

"Two days of heaven, and then . . . nothing," he said.

"You can't stay here for two days," I said. "I won't father this damned imposture for another moment."

"I'll move to the inn, sir," said Terry. Of course, he could not do that.

I said: "Stop 'sirring' me . . . and go to bed . . . and be damned!"

"Yes, sir," said Terry.

It is difficult for me to record the happenings of the next two days because the mind turns from pain and from shame, but I cannot rub out of my brain the voice of Terry—he had a squawking baritone that lacked both the high notes and the low—as he roamed through the house singing. He was so happy that the servants loved him, but whenever he saw me, his manner changed abruptly. He was like a frightened rabbit. Naturally I saw very little of him because most of the time he was at the Casimir-Jones house with Elena, reading poetry aloud to her . . . or taking riding lessons. In the meantime, I avoided all society and refused to answer the telephone; the *honk* of an automobile on the nearest highway sent echoes of fear through me because I felt that a neighbor might be coming to call.

It was not until Sunday afternoon that Barry Casimir-Jones sent me the following note:

Dear Jack:

I have tried to get you on the phone half a dozen times. You're not running out on me in the pinch, are you? Elena is completely dizzy about young Barnes. He makes me a bit crazy, too, but not in just the same way. He's coming over here for supper tonight, and I'll expect you with him, without fail. Things are getting a bit thick. I think you know what I mean.

I saw, in fact, that I would have to show my face again in public, so I drove over with Terry, merely saying to him on the way: "Your two days of heaven are over, my lad. Tomorrow you leave. That will end my agreement with you, I believe."

He took the decision in a sick silence that lasted until he got to the house of Casimir-Jones. He was wearing riding togs, which I thought rather odd for Sunday supper, until Elena met him at the house and took him in tow at once. She had just the horse for him to take a lesson on, she said, and fetched him off at once toward the stable. They walked arm in arm, the girl laughing up at him as they chattered. As I looked after them, I felt a dash lonely, for, of course, I could not tell how the sky was to fall on both their heads before the evening was ended.

These Sunday suppers at the Casimir-Jones place had been fixtures since Elena was a twelve-year-old. A score of her intimates were sure to turn up together with a few friends of her parents. After Elsie Casimir-Jones died, Barry continued the parties as a matter of habit. This Sunday only a few of the early birds had arrived before us, so that Elena was able to excuse herself to give the riding lesson. Also, I was able to have a few words with Barry.

He said: "This is serious, Jack. It's no filly and colt affair. The poor gal trembles when she speaks his name."

I answered him: "Tomorrow, the whole thing will go up in a puff of smoke. Now stop thinking about it and don't ask me any questions."

He looked hard at me for a moment before he said: "Very well. I'll let it go at that."

"You let it go at that," I told him, and turned to look out the window.

The sun was not down and a pale moon was rising over the stables, which stand very close to the Casimir-Jones house, a convenience most places do without. I cannot hold with the oversensitive people who are afraid to be to leeward of a barn and I enjoyed, at that moment, the big, honest face of the stables with the weathercock jaunting on one foot above the roof. There were the pastures, too, with the last warmth of the sun on a field from which the brood mares and their foals were being driven toward the barn. In a nearer paddock Terry Barnes was riding an old brown gelding around and around the enclosure while Elena leaned at the fence and gave advice. They were not close enough for me to study the faces, but I could see how the impatient young rascal allowed his elbows to flop and his knees to loosen. Inside the adjoining fence, a groom was leading beautiful Starboard around and around in circles, with a sack of oats tied in the saddle.

"Why don't you give up the brute?" I asked Barry.

"Why not before he outright kills someone? He'd have a value in the stud, what with his bloodlines and all. You'll never make him tractable that way . . . he has to be ridden and ridden out before he'll be worth a hang."

"I know it," said Barry. "But why not ask Elena to give up the pound of flesh nearest her heart? Remember that Starboard belongs to her. She gentled him. He used to play with her like a dog when he was a yearling. He'll still follow her about. She can do anything except sit on his back, and she keeps hoping that the time will come. It's one of those hopeless things. Like death to me, Jack, every time I think of that wastage."

People began to pour in, at about this time, and Elena came back to the house. She found a dozen of her friends at the windows, laughing at Terry on the old horse. It was amazing to see the way she faced them down, blooming with enthusiasm. She cried out: "You'll see! He'll make a fine rider, someday. He has rhythm in him. That's what makes a horseman, or a *poet!*"

Their laughter passed into feeble smiling.

Her father said: "By the way, does Terry Barnes ever talk about any poet except that Chinaman, Tu Fu?"

This turned her blank, for a moment, but she murmured: "No . . . I don't think so. . . . But that's the way a great enthusiasm is. It eats up all the little things."

I had a grim hope that Barry might pursue the theme he had opened up, but he had struck on it only by chance and he let it drop. The big room was buzzing with talk now, for nearly everyone had come in. The sun had set; there was more moon than daylight to show Terry still jogging his gelding and the groom still patiently walking the stallion.

I happened to be watching from a window when Elena paused beside me and said: "Isn't Terry patient? He's so. . . ."

"What?" I snapped, and dimmed her happiness a bit.

"So tractable," she finished, and went back among her guests.

A moment later, Terence came into the room and Elena attached herself to him with a rather sickly smile. It was at this instant that I heard Dyke Vincent exclaim something that was chiefly wordless but that had a damn or two worked into the woof.

When he felt my eye on him, he muttered: "I never heard such a lot of maundering rot. Uncle Jack, will you come over with me and see if she's really out of her mind, or not, sir?"

I went over with Dyke. By the red of his neck I knew that he was not in a fit frame of mind to talk to a girl. He got Elena into a corner with me and said: "Now you talk turkey, Elena, will you?"

"Are you going to be a silly idiot about something, Dyke?" she asked.

"I don't know what you call silly," said Vincent. "That's why I want Mister Whitlock to be the judge."

She gave me her hand and her smile. She had as sweet a way about her as a yearling filly that's never felt a strap.

"Speaking of silly," said Dyke, "is that damned Tu Fu anything else?"

"Dyke, you're speaking of one of the world's great poets," said Elena.

"Yeah, he's God, I guess," said Dyke. "And that cock-eyed, slab-sided four-flusher of a Barnes is the prophet, I suppose?"

"Steady, Dyke," I warned. "There's no use spurring downhill, you know."

"I've had quite enough of this . . . are you boiled, Dyke?" she asked, and started to leave.

But I touched her arm and she remained.

"I think Dyke has something to say," I told her.

"Buckets full," said Vincent. "I've been looking you over. I'll tell you what you need. The same thing that Starboard ought to have. A master . . . and I'm not going to talk any more. I'm going to do something about it."

It was rather strong talk. It left me a bit dazed as Dyke turned on his heel and stalked away from us. I hardened myself to endure an outburst from Elena, but she amazed me by saying: "Dyke is rather sweet, isn't he?"

"*Ha!*" I said. "Sweet?"

Then another thought came to me, and I added: "Do you think the foolish fellow is going out to ride Starboard now?"

Certainly I should have understood before and kept Dyke from leaving the room. I heard the words and the name of the horse; I knew perfectly well that Starboard was a savage devil, and that, while he might be handled in the muck of a plowed field, he never should be attempted in a narrow paddock in the dusk of the day, but, although I knew these things, poor Dyke was well out of the room before I hitched things together. Then I started after him, saying to Casimir-Jones as I passed him: "I'm afraid Vincent is going to try Starboard. He has to be stopped." Unfortunately I said it loudly enough to reach every ear in the room, so that, as Barry and I hurried out toward the paddock, everyone else was following along.

We came up in time to see Dyke settle into the saddle as the groom loosed the head of Starboard. Elena was running forward, crying out something.

I shouted: "Dyke! Dyke! Get off that horse!" Then as Terry came panting up beside me, I added to him: "If that brute murders Vincent, you and your damned Tu Fu are to blame for it."

Everybody was babbling; I heard Elena shrilling a protest; then the hoofs of Starboard beat the breath out of us, and we were still. It was horrible to watch. The stallion fought like a cat, not like honest horseflesh. He rubbed Dyke loose against the fence, and then flung him like a stone out of the saddle. I hoped for an instant that the stone would keep on rolling until it reached safety under the lowest bar of the fence, but poor Dyke wound up in a tumbled heap well inside the paddock with big Starboard coming at him like a devil. I heard Casimir-Jones screeching: "Who has a gun? Who has a gun?" Then I saw Terry Barnes run in between Dyke and the horse.

In the quiet of retrospect I can see that a lad with Terry's blood would feel a compulsion to do such a thing, but at the moment the pictures moved too quickly for me to think at all. The eye got ahead of the brain, so to speak. In that bewildering flicker of images I saw Starboard rear to strike down Terry, and the next bit of the film showed the boy dodging the hoofs and getting, by miracle, into the saddle. Starboard answered by going right over backward.

The end of the day gave a filthy light, the light for a murder, you might say, and I did not make out exactly what happened, except that when Starboard got to his feet again, a rag of humanity was still in the saddle. The moon and the sunset showed us Terry's face streaming with blood.

Starboard soared among the stars again and came down on the other side of the paddock fence with such a shock that the rider whip-snapped in the saddle. It made me inches smaller to see what happened to him. Then I heard Casimir-Jones shouting something and saw a gun in his hand. I gripped it and yelled in his ear that his bullet was as apt to hit the rider as the horse.

It was a tremendous thing to watch, that battle. Even the women stopped screeching, after an instant, and huddled closer to the fence while Starboard danced between the sky and the earth. That brute would hit the stars and leave sparks in my eyes and then bang the ground with a force that made me shiver. At last he raced right down the slope.

"The creek . . . and the wall!" shouted Casimir-Jones.

We heard the *crash* of the horse in the water.

"That's the end," said Casimir-Jones, starting to climb through the fence. But then the beat of hoofs began again and we looked, expecting to see a riderless horse fly over the farther ridge, but, when the silhouette appeared, the rider was still in place, a senseless weight that swung from side to side.

Then we were silent again.

Elena Casimir-Jones was superintending the lifting of Dyke Vincent from the ground, but as soon as the good fellow felt his feet under him, he came back to his senses. I heard him ask what had happened.

Young Tillinghast answered: "That Terry Barnes, who was learning to ride . . . he ran in and kept Starboard from savaging you . . . he's riding Starboard now, unless he's dead in a ditch."

The daylight was gone. There were the moon and the stars and all of us waiting silently in the shadows. When anyone spoke, it was in a murmur. Elena whispered at my shoulder: "Uncle Jack, did you know about him all the time? *Will* he come back alive?"

I chose to answer only the second question and to lie about it. I remembered the helplessly swinging figure that Starboard had carried over the black rim of the hill, but I said: "He's a Barnes . . . of course, he'll come back."

When I got my breath, after that, I explained: "He thought he had to be different from the rest. He thought. . . ."

"I know," said Elena, and leaned her head against my shoulder. However, she did not weep, for the Casimir-Jones strain is purest thoroughbred.

I heard her father say: "I should have destroyed Starboard long ago. I want everyone to know that I take full responsibility for this. . . ."

"Wait a minute! What's that?" called someone.

Then I heard a horse trotting down the lane behind the house toward the stables. It came into view from among the trees a moment later, a downheaded, beaten horse with the rider bowed far over in the saddle.

"It's Starboard," I muttered.

Here Elena came alive suddenly and ran off crying: "Terry! Terry! Terry!"

The rest of us hurried on fast enough to see Terry Barnes slip out of the saddle and lean drunkenly, staggering against the shoulder of the stallion. Starboard had had his bellyful of fighting, at last. The moon was full on Terry's face and it was not a pretty thing to see. His clothes were ripped to rags and more than cloth had been torn; yet being of the Barnes-Whitlock strain, he managed to walk to the house with little help, although he collapsed inside the door. I remember poor Elena with an arm under his head, crying up to us: "Will he die? Will he die?"

Of course, a fellow with such bloodlines was bound to pull through. He and Elena make a happy pair. There is only one subject for silence in their house: poetry and poets are taboo.

Sign of the Hawk

Ten short novels and ten serials written by Frederick Faust appeared in 1930. All but "Sign of the Hawk" were published in Street & Smith's *Western Story Magazine*, which probably was due to Faust's sympathetic portrayal of the hero, Ching Wo, who has been raised Chinese. The story, which Faust had finished in June 1930 and titled "Wild Honey", appeared in *Railroad Man's Magazine*, a Frank A. Munsey publication, and was run in six parts in the issues from August 30, 1930 through January 31, 1931. For its appearance here, the serial has been restored according to the author's original typescript.

I

In the days before the Union Pacific cut its iron way across the continent, the sole means of communication with undeveloped sections of the West consisted of horseback riders, covered wagons, stagecoaches, and riverboats.

One of the most famous of those boats, the *Prairie Belle*, was swinging around a wide, easy corner of the Sacramento and coming into a great shallows, where the water was so still that all of a sunset cloud lay upon its face. Beside this reflected glory the central current of the river ran with only a dim ripple.

Entering the easy going, the steam engine instantly gathered speed, the old river boat trembled with the throb of power, and the paddle wheel under the stern dashed on with renewed energy.

In spite of the increased noise of the engine and the wheel, however, the *Prairie Belle* was fairly quiet. For the whole of the noise-making elements of the passenger list were gathered into the smoking room, where they had been playing poker since they left San Francisco, and where a crooked gambler's more crooked faro box was also heavily patronized.

They had been drinking, too, filling themselves with whiskey and wines that had been carted in swift clipper ships from Boston, New York, and New Orleans, all the dreary, wild journey around the Horn.

Some of those champagnes that were opened for the card players on the *Prairie Belle* were worth almost their weight in gold dust. But of dust, there was plenty, and even though the money belts of some of the players were almost empty, they were going into the regions where gold was easily washed from the earth, or where the gullible golddiggers could easily be looted by cleverer minds.

All of the noise and merriment were confined to the cabin, however, and the voices that arose there after a big play came only dimly out onto the prow of the boat, where a great many of the poorer passengers were collected.

Here, too, there had been dice games on the deck. A mandolin had been trembling out its music in the hands of a Mexican seated on an apple barrel near the port rail. But the games had ceased, and the mandolin was still as the prow of the ship cut into the heart of the reflected cloud upon the water. For now the passengers had begun to look out over the marshes and plains bordering the Sacramento River.

On either side the tules stood tall and thick. And where the solid ground came down to the water's edge, some cattle lifted their dripping muzzles and watched the ship go by. Not long before, such a sight would have sent the half-wild creatures frantic with fear—as locomotives were destined to do some years later—but now it was long since they had grown accustomed to the steady procession of fire canoes that worked up the river toward the gold fields.

Beyond tules and cattle extended the darkening flat of the plains, dimly streaked here and there with the oaks that grew along the sloughs and looked, in this half light, like undulations of smoke.

Two Chinamen, standing together by the starboard rail of the *Prairie Belle*, imitated the silence of all the whites until, the sunset fading still more, dice games were resumed, the mandolin began its song again, and patches of conversation sprang up here and there. Then Fow Ming spoke.

For a Chinaman he was very big—nearly six feet, and with the shoulders and grim face of a warrior. A jagged scar on the right cheek made him appear yet more resolute and formidable.

Said Fow Ming: "We are riding on a dragon's back, my friend. There is fire in its belly, smoke in its nostrils, and its voice is a groan."

Li Wo made soft answer: "It is going, also, into what the white men consider heaven, but which you will find closer to their hell."

Their native tongue aroused the antagonism of a great sullen-faced boor, who gripped Li Wo by the shoulder and thrust him roughly away.

"You damn' chinks, stop your yappin', if you can't talk a white man's lingo."

The teeth of Fow Ming set with a *click*, but Li Wo hastily caught his arm and drew him forward, nearer to the prow.

"He has lost at faro," Li Wo explained, "and he's only waiting for an excuse to cut our throats."

"I, also, carry a knife," said Fow Ming.

"Good," Li Wo responded, "but every man's hand is against us. If we strike back, we are dead."

"It is better to die than to be dishonored," Fow Ming growled savagely.

"What did the Great Teacher say?" quoted Li. " 'In every man's country, follow his customs.' "

"What customs are they?" said Fow Ming. "These men are barbarians. They are as low as coolies in our own country. They are lower still. They are neither well born nor well taught, nor do they have the manners of gentlemen.

"I know them . . . I know them," Fow Ming added after a pause. "I have lived in San Francisco long enough to understand them. We must go with our heads continually bowed. I have seen our brothers struck in the face because they dared to look up."

"It is not you and I who have taught them to hate us," said Li Wo. "But the honest, hard-working coolies have made them angry."

"That I understand. But how?"

"Because in the mines the white laborers eat meat three times a day, and drink a great deal of coffee. Once a week they must make themselves drunk with bad whiskey. And men with such habits must have high wages. Against them, consider the coolies. Twice a day they sit down with a bowl of rice and a little fat in it for seasoning. When they have eaten that, they are contented. They can work for a quarter of what the white man must have. And the money they make, they save."

"They save," said Fow Ming, "until the white devils murder and rob them and take their money away!"

"True," said Li Wo. "They are murdered and robbed, at times. But still the number of Chinamen increases. More and more of the gold sticks to their hands. You will find our countrymen who have gained in one year enough to take them back to China and keep them wealthy the remainder of their lives."

Fow Ming sighed. "May the day soon come when I go over the ocean once more."

The other, overcome with his anger, did not speak for a time, but regarded the darkening face of the water.

Meanwhile, from the smoke room, a slender young man came sauntering forward with a fumbling step, as though more than two-thirds mastered by liquor. He sang in a faint, stumbling voice and laughed a little at his own errors.

"Look well, Li Wo," said Fow Ming. "There is a gambler or a gentleman. I can tell by his clothes."

A deck lamp had gleamed upon the gaudy pattern of the fellow's waistcoat, upon his tall, white hat, upon the diamond in his neck cloth.

"Who would debase himself in the eye of the whole world?" inquired Li Wo. "Oh, my friend, that we should have to cringe before such creatures."

The youth had gone straight to the tip of the prow, as though he were going to walk on into the river. No one attempted to stop him. No one gave him advice. He was allowed to stand there on the verge, teetering perilously back and forth.

The rest of the passengers of the deck began to laugh.

"I'll bet fifty dollars against a hundred that he falls in," volunteered one gambler.

The same ruffian who already had manhandled the Chinaman now strode out to have a better look. "I wouldn't take you for more'n even money."

"I'll give you three to five," persisted the first man. "That's odds enough for you, Charlie."

"Why," began Charlie, and then, as he turned to answer, his foot struck the baggage of Li Wo, a rounded bundle wrapped in stout cloth. Charlie, stumbling over this obstacle, no sooner saw what it was than he burst into a curse and snatched it up.

"They ain't room in the world for me an' two chinks," he said. "Go after it, you rat, if you want it!"

He scooped up the bundle and was about to hurl it over the rail when Fow Ming checked his hand.

There was power in the Oriental's arm, and Charlie's grip was broken.

He staggered, the bundle coming out of his hand and remaining in that of the big Chinaman.

At this, Charlie became so furious that he could not speak; he uttered a sort of screeching cry. It caused all hands to turn toward him. Even the youthful drunkard at the prow began to ramble unevenly toward the scene.

"Look!" yelled Charlie. "I'm handled an' manhandled by a pair of lousy damn' chinks! Why, I'm gonna cut the kidneys out of the pair of 'em. I'm gonna. . . ."

His voice ended in another inarticulate shout of rage. Not a soul stirred to stop him in his rush, although the great, gleaming Bowie knife in his hand showed that he meant business even as he had promised it. But the life of a Chinaman, as Fow Ming and Li Wo had already said, was worth no more than the life of a dog in the California of the gold rush days. They stood by, and on more than one brutal face appeared a gaping grin of expectation as the bully charged.

Chance, however, had brought the tipsy youngster back from the prow, and he reeled into Charlie's path. There, floundering to get away from the charge, his feet became entangled in the legs of Charlie, but it was the latter who fell heavily, the Bowie knife spinning out of his hand.

II

Both Fow Ming and his slenderer companion had stood still in the presence of the charge, with faces like two yellow masks. When the knife rattled at his feet, Fow Ming's eye glinted like the eyes of a snake, and a ghost of a smile tugged at the corners of his mouth.

But Charlie was down, not out. He came to his feet in a foaming frenzy.

First he looked wildly about him for the fallen knife, but one of the soft-soled shoes of Fow Ming now covered it. Then he stared at the Chinamen, lurched a little toward them, and finally decided that the white youth must come first.

"I'm gonna sober you!" he bellowed to the boy. "I'm gonna bust you in two an' drop the pieces into the river." Charlie's fists clenched.

The youngster, in the meantime, had not sought to flee, but remained nearby, wavering a little from the perpendicular from time to time, but apparently without fear. He showed a dark, finely cut face, and an olive skin, almost like that of a Mexican; a Mexican's black eyes, too, were fixed good-naturedly upon Charlie while he answered: "Frightfully sorry, old fellow. Wouldn't have tripped you up for the world."

"You lie, damn you!" yelled Charlie, and started forward.

The drunkard did not move. With hands dropped lightly into the pockets of his coat, he remained staggeringly in place, watching the charge of the big fellow.

Yet the first rush did not succeed. Perhaps it was the tremor that ran through the ship as it nosed again into the heart of the current at the next bend that threw the tipsy boy off balance. At any rate, he reeled suddenly to the side as Charlie, floundering past him, whirled again, red-eyed as a bull, and bellowing as loudly. His face frightful to see, but a frightened voice yelled:

"Charlie! Hey, you fool! It's Delancey! It's Handsome Harry!"

The effect upon the ruffian was like that of a whip stroke fairly across the face. He checked his own rush, and with such suddenness that he almost fell.

"Handsome Harry!" he gasped. "Oh, my God!"

Shrinking inches from his former stature, he slunk off into the crowd and was gone.

Handsome Harry remained in the midst of the deck, surrounded by a respectful silence and many bright, curious eyes. For a moment he faltered there, then made his slow, uncertain way aft again, murmuring: "Dreadfully sorry . . . wouldn't have dreamed . . . shocking affair . . . dear me, dear me."

The passengers drew a little back to either side and gave him an easy way aft. After he had gone, it seemed that everyone breathed more freely.

As for the Chinamen, Fow Ming rolled his eyes in a single expressive glance at Li Wo, who glanced back. That was all. It was not until long minutes afterward that Fow Ming, stooping, gathered the long, bright blade of the Bowie knife up the sleeve of his silk coat and passed his sensitive fingers along the haft, rudely indented by three notches.

The interruption had stopped all talk except for a few murmurs that began to rise, here and there.

One strapping youth inquired softly of his companion: "Who's Handsome Harry?"

"Well, who you think, tenderfoot?" responded the other.

"Why, you'd think he was gunpowder, with a lighted fuse buried in it."

"Well, he is, kid."

"One of those killers, eh?"

"Him? Handsome Harry?"

"Yes."

"Listen to me, son," explained the older man, "when it comes to a gent like Handsome Harry, the best thing in the world is for you to keep your face shut. Don't go askin' questions, even. Just pick up information here an' there. That's what I mean to say."

"Only," said the youngster, "I'd like to know why it is, if he's a murderer, that he ain't arrested right quick."

"Who'd arrest him?" said the other. "Is there men enough aboard? I dunno. I wouldn't make one of the crowd that tried it. Not unless they was ten ranks deep an' me in the last rank. Who would it pay to arrest him?"

"Well, but there's a sheriff aboard, ain't there?"

"Callin' a man a sheriff don't make him shoot no straighter. Besides, they ain't apt to be no warrant out for Harry. A slick gent like him, he never shoots till the other sucker has filled his hand. An' after that, it's self-defense, ain't it?"

"You mean he's so fast he can wait?"

"That's what I don't mean nothin' else. Look at him, drunk like he was, an' still Charlie Jennings couldn't lay a hand on him. An' Charlie's a fightin' man, too. Don't make no mistake about that."

"He was pretty quick scared."

"Naw, he just pretty quick got sense, that was all."

They talked of other things, and Fow Ming said softly to his friend: "Oh, Li Wo, no matter how drunk, that youth is a man, is he not?"

"He is," said Li Wo.

48

"And a warrior."

"Yes."

"Perhaps a gentleman, too, after the ways of this wild country?"

"Yes," said Li Wo.

"Do you know of him?"

"What is there to know?" responded Li Wo. "We hear of him now and then. Men love to talk of such a man as Handsome Harry Delancey, but no man sees him twice. No ear hears him twice. Look. One man on this boat knew him, and that one man is now hiding in a dark corner like a mouse, I am sure, and wishing he had let Charlie Jennings die."

"To be so fatal," said Fow Ming, with great interest, "he is very young, is he not?"

"Into the brains of some men wisdom is put . . . into the hands of some men wisdom is put. The wits of Handsome Harry are not stupid. Neither are his hands." Li Wo pointed before him. "There is the city in which my house stands, Fow Ming. There is Buffalo Flat."

Beyond the bend, seen through the willows that here lined the high bank of the stream, appeared the lights of a town that grew brighter and thicker as they drew near, and at last they could see the whole place spread before them.

"Down from that river," continued Li Wo, "come the miners with their gold dust from the mines. More of them come, also, from higher up the Sacramento. Here they stop, usually. Here they enjoy their first taste of the gold they have dug, and here they leave a great share of it. A man with a filled purse does not stop eating until he has forgotten hunger."

They laughed a little together, very softly, as the boat slipped into its mooring. A shouting crowd was on the bank. Other voices yelled from the steamer, and soon the gangplank was run out and the people flooded down.

"We wait until the last," said Fow Ming bitterly. "Even the Negroes go down before us."

So it was that they stood by and watched the others descend. And among the rest, Charlie Jennings, striding through the crowd, cast a black look upon them and went on.

"That man," Fow Ming remarked, "wishes his knife were in our hearts. And the edge of his knife is sharp . . . I am thumbing it now."

He smiled at Li Wo, who answered rather carelessly: "I am not without a shelter in time of need, friend. Let us go on without fear."

They took their bundles down the gangplank when their turn at last came. Slipping out of the crowd, they circled the busy end of the Main Street and went down to the side of the town.

At last they came to a little hump-backed bridge across an insignificant slough that emptied into the Sacramento, and in the center of the bridge Li Wo paused.

"There is the American city behind us, my friend. On the farther side we come to our own country. There is only a little of it. But the color of heaven is still blue, even though it has fallen into a duck pond. In that town I hope to make you welcome. I hope to make you comfortable for a few days."

"And can you make me safe?" Fow Ming asked curiously. "Do the Americans stay away from the place?"

"Who can keep them out?" responded Li Wo gloomily. "Sometimes the wild young men come on their horses and ride up and down the streets, shooting. It is not twenty days since a good man was murdered as he sat at the door of his house. He was shot by a wild young fool, who killed, not in malice, but for the sake of the noise his gun made."

Fow Ming drew in his breath through expanded nostrils, but at length he said grimly: "We are being followed. Let us hurry on across the bridge. Let us get to safety among your own people. For the brute is at our heels once more."

Li Wo looked back, and saw that burly Charlie Jennings was not far behind them at the beginning of the little bridge. He started on at once, murmuring: "Quickly, but not too quickly, my friend. If we run, he will commence shooting, and, if he were to kill us before the very door of my house, not one of my neighbors would dare to stop him, or to revenge us."

III

That unpleasant suggestion did not make Fow Ming hasten or falter in his gait, but he went on with a regular step, although the shadow of the head and shoulders of Charlie Jennings now began to play about the feet of the fugitives, as he swept down from the crown of the bridge.

But the faces of the two Chinamen masked the utmost agony of spirit, for they knew what lay before them. To resist was probably to die. They would be lucky if they escaped with merely a beating and mockery and humiliation. Both of them could remember horrible sights of their countrymen with queues tied together being dragged at the heels of horses, or forced to drag carts like beasts of burden.

Such things might happen to them, now, at the fancy of Charlie Jennings, and, if they resisted, they were sure to bring down upon their own section of the town the wrath of the white city across the slough.

"He is on us," said Li Wo, a spasm of horror convulsing his face.

Suddenly the long arm of Jennings reached out behind them and fastened on Li's shoulder, jerked him around, and then crashed him against the railing of the bridge.

With beastly joy Charlie Jennings studied the lithe Chinaman, the calm, undaunted face, the lowered eyes that still sought to turn away wrath by giving no offense, by indicating neither fear nor contempt.

"I'm gonna teach you somethin'," said Charlie Jennings. "I'm gonna teach you what a white man's fist tastes like, an' after that you can dive over the rail an' drink slough soup. Why, I'm gonna teach you manners, that's what I'm gonna do, you yaller pigs! I'm gonna teach the two of you."

He ended with a burst of furious satisfaction, for he saw that Fow Ming was standing motionlessly by. He would not have been so delighted if he had known that one of Fow Ming's sleeve-hidden hands was now gripping hard the handle of Charlie's Bowie knife.

As he turned upon Fow Ming, he saw another form come lightly up the arch of the bridge from the Chinese section of the town toward the white. But it was no Oriental. There was something familiar about that figure, and about the light, fumbling step.

He hesitated one more instant, then the slender youth stopped, and he heard the genial voice of Handsome Harry Delancey crying: "Why, here you are again, Charlie Jennings! Here you are again. I'm glad to see you!"

The words were cheerful. There was nothing but friendliness in the voice, and yet Jennings was filled with doubt. He merely growled: "Here's a pair of sneakin' chinks that've stole my knife, between 'em, an' that are laughin' up their sleeves at all of the white gents in the world. I wanna ask you, are we gonna stand for that, old-timer? Are we gonna stand for that, Harry, or are we gonna teach 'em a lesson right here an' now?"

"Ah, but, Charlie," said Handsome Harry, "you're a little young to be a teacher, don't you think? Just a little young . . . and out late at night, too . . . terribly late at night. Don't you think I ought to take you home?"

There was no doubting the attitude that lay beneath his smiling exterior, and Charlie Jennings stared at the newcomer with the most earnest hatred. He wanted more than all things to go for his gun and blow this persecutor off the bridge.

He would have paid down ten years of life for such a delight, as a matter of fact, but now it seemed to Charlie that he was looking at the very face and form of a smiling death as he surveyed young Harry Delancey.

Charlie Jennings backed up. He forgot the two Chinamen altogether, and then, spinning about, he bolted at full speed over the arch of the bridge. He much preferred life to honor.

Handsome Harry did not run in pursuit, but laughed a little in wicked enjoyment. Then he sauntered forward without so much as a glance toward the two Orientals.

"Let's go on," Li Wo suggested.

"And leave him without a word of thanks?" said Fow Ming. "By my honorable fathers, I am not a worthy man if I do not go to thank him for something that is worth more to me than life."

"And have him spit in your face?" asked Li Wo. "That is how he would answer. I know these people.

To him, that brave young man, we are no more than a pair of dogs."

"Are you sure?"

"I am sure."

"There is a curse on these people, then," said Fow Ming sullenly. "Let us hurry on, now. I am a little sick at heart,"

They went onward, therefore, through the entanglement of twisting streets that all were silent and empty now, except for an occasional householder seated at the door of his shop or house, puffing at a long-stemmed pipe. The houses were of the flimsiest construction, huddled together in heaps and looking as though they needed their mutual support in order to keep from collapsing. Most of the windows were now shuttered so as to keep light in and the air out.

A solitary voice made the rest of the silence more unendurable, but neither Fow Ming nor Li Wo spoke of it as they journeyed on. It was too bitter to them. It was the shadow of the dominant race that silenced their people like the shadow of a sailing hawk.

They came, at last, to a street that ended against the river embankment, and at the end of the street there was a house with open street door, and a squatting figure smoking a pipe there.

"That is my house," said Li Wo.

As they came to it, the doorkeeper stood up and moved a little to the side, then bowed low to them. They passed up some *creaking* steps and through a number of little, wretched rooms, very dirty and in disorder so great that Fow Ming looked straight before him, and studied to keep the contempt from appearing in his face.

Li Wo had guided them by the light of a dim lantern taken from the first room, and now he raised the lantern above his head and scrutinized a strong brick wall—such as might be built to retain the river embankment. In the center of this wall he tapped twice, paused, and tapped rapidly three times again.

At once a narrow section swung outward. The servant who had opened the hidden door backed away, bowing deeply.

Across this threshold, Fow Ming found himself in a different world. A faint and unearthly fragrance hung in the air, without making it heavy. Soft lights illumined the rooms, and he had a sense of flowers everywhere about him.

They passed a curtained entrance, and, when Li Wo drew the curtain aside, Fow Ming saw a tiny chamber with a weird little seated Buddha at the farther end of it, between two columns, and in front of the idol burned a pair of candles. It was these that poured the fragrance through the house. Fow Ming recognized that scent and knew it was of great price.

The curtain fell across the face of the god, and they went on. Every room was small but pleasantly furnished. Clean mattings covered the floors; screens of flowered work sheltered the doorways. Suddenly they came out upon a little rock garden fenced with a lofty stone wall on either side. It covered the top of the river embankment, screened from it by thick willows and poplars planted in a row, and yet through the trees one could make out the glint of the black face of the water.

The lantern that the master of the house had carried was now taken from him by one servant. Others approached with new and pleasanter lights, screened by shades of painted paper so that they looked like beautiful, self-illumined butterflies. These were hung here and there so that the light they shed would not glare in the eyes of host or guest. A new, delicate aroma filled the air. Fow Ming guessed that the light was given by costly, scented candles even like those that burned before the face of the Buddha.

In the meantime, rugs were swiftly brought, unrolled, and cushions placed upon them. Covered cups of guest tea were brought, and all was managed in such silence and with such speed that it was like domestic magic. Fow Ming knew a well-ordered household when he saw one, and he looked with a new respect upon the dapper little man who sat with him.

Then food began to appear for the evening meal, and it was a feast. First soup made of sea slugs. Then chicken minced soft and flavored with pork. Next came flour balls cooked in sugar, fish brains, a wonderful dish composed solely of the tongues of ducks, and at least a dozen confections, beginning with candied bamboo root.

The two Chinamen drank with this meal rice wine, at first, and afterward hot *samshu*, in little bowls.

After the meal had ended, pipes were brought and

lighted with glowing coals. The men reclined at ease, puffing at clumsy mouthpieces and watching silver fluctuations of the fountain that played in the center of the little garden. The evening air was warm and still, stars stood low in the sky, and from the farther side of the embankment they could hear the continual lapping of water.

In this time of tranquility, Fow Ming looked into his knowledge of his friend and his heart was softened. His daughter had been demanded by Li Wo for marriage with young Ching Wo. But she was Fow's only child, and Fow hated the thought of parting with her. So he had come down the river to visit the household of his friend, according to the proverb that he now repeated.

"Li Wo, the face of a man may be silent, but the house of a man is never done speaking. Everything that I have seen is pleasant. But why do you not let me see your son?"

IV

It was the question which, of course, Li Wo had been awaiting for a long time, but now he put the thing away, as in courtesy bound.

For he said: "Your politeness, my friend, has two right hands. But I cannot allow you to see the boy now when you are tired and are thinking only of sleep."

"If he is here, let him come in," was Fow Ming's response.

Li touched a gong, rubbing it with the tips of his fingers, and bringing a faint *hum* of music from the thin metal. Instantly a servant slipped from the shadows and stood before him.

"Is my son here?"

"He is here. He has been here for an hour."

"How is he occupied now?"

"As always at this time, he is studying."

"Tell him to come to me at once."

The servant disappeared. And Fow Ming questioned: "May I speak to you freely, friend?"

"Speak to me freely," said Li Wo. "If you are to become his second father, you should know him as well as I can teach you."

"Then," said Fow, "it appears to me that a young man should find his place in his home every day. Does he wander out at night by himself?"

"He goes often down the river to the house of a friend, who is a great teacher. That is where he has been for the last few days, while I was in San Francisco."

"He is a student, then?"

"He will one day be a distinguished scholar," said Li Wo, with a flash entering his eye.

"And he studies when he returns to his house?"

"He studies here, also."

"This steals a boy's health," Fow Ming remarked. "But here he comes."

Ching Wo, the son of Li, came slowly into the garden, bowed very low before his father, and remained bowed until Li spoke a careless word. After that he greeted the guest, and then drew back a little and remained with his head slightly dropped.

He looked like what his father had called him—a scholar. It seemed that a confined life had made him very pale, so that, for the color of his skin, he might have passed for an Italian as well as for a Chinaman. He was a handsome youngster, even by Western standards, with just a touch of weariness in his eyes.

The young man was told to sit down, and he obeyed in silence, keeping his eyes so fixed upon the floor that Fow Ming was able to turn upon Li Wo a glance expressive of his open admiration.

"How is it," Fow Ming asked the boy, "that you stay so much in your father's house, when there is such a great world outside of it?"

The boy looked up, but at his father, not at the guest.

"You may answer him," said Li Wo.

"Without going out of doors, we can know the whole world," replied Ching Wo.

"*Ha!*" Fow Ming started a little. "What is it you say?"

"They are not my words," answered the boy. "They are the words of Lao Tzu."

"Do you know many of his words, my son?" asked Fow Ming, looking steadily at the youngster.

"A great sun may shine through a narrow window," was the reply, "and a small bird may listen to the river flowing."

Said Fow Ming: "If you live only with teachers and

books, it will be hard for you to find a place for your-self in the world."

"If I have learned patience," the boy answered, "per-haps it will help me when I must begin to work in the world."

"Patience is a great strength," agreed Fow Ming, "but there are some things, perhaps, which can be learned only with force. Like the handling of nettles are some problems in life, my son."

"If that is so," said the boy, "I shall be glad to know how to do such things as you describe."

Fow Ming regarded him with an open nod of approval. "And your books have given you some ambition in the world, Ching Wo? You wish to be a rich prince, I suppose?"

"I wish to be a merchant," answered Ching Wo. "It is my father's wish."

"*Ha!*" said the visitor. "Are his wishes yours?"

The boy lifted his head a little. "I am his son."

The other nodded, and began to cough a little, as though to cover a momentary embarrassment.

"Is that all?" asked the son.

"It is sufficient," said Li Wo. "You are tired," he added, "and therefore you may go to your bed at once."

With bows as profound as those with which he had entered, Ching Wo departed again from the garden, moving backward like a courtier from the presence of a king, until he was in the shadow of the house, and then noiselessly disappearing.

Fow Ming inquired with a smile: "Are you an emperor, Li Wo, and is that one of your slaves?"

At this moment there was a sudden outburst of guns firing up the river in the main portion of the town of Buffalo Flat. As the shooting died down, they heard plainly a single voice raised in a long, pealing screech of terror and pain.

Fow Ming started to his feet, but, instantly recovering himself, sat down again. Then he remarked to his impassive host by way of apology for his lack of self-control: "After I had talked to your son, it seemed to me, Li Wo, that we were all back in the kingdom of beauty and of peace, our own country, and the guns and the cry were like the sudden work of dragons in your garden. Well . . . in what way have you managed to raise such a son in such a country, where the fools and the barbarians are all about him?"

"By patience." An almost evil exultation came into Li Wo's face. "From the day of his birth I have worked to make him what I would have him be. The labor is not quite finished, but at least I think you can see him as he will be."

Fow Ming responded with enthusiasm: "I never have seen a young man who seemed more virtuous. It is only possible that he is too delicate. Yet I see that his fingernails are not long."

"That is true," answered Li Wo. "His fingernails are not long. I intend him to be a merchant. I intend that he shall sail many oceans. Therefore, I have taught him to grow up, expecting no life of books in the future, even if he should begin with many books now. He is to work, even with his hands when his life depends upon them."

At this, Fow Ming made a gesture with both hands, sweeping outward. "Li Wo, I expected to stay here many days, studying your son and trying to learn what his heart might be, but I think I have seen enough to please me forever. If you still are willing, he shall be my daughter's husband."

"Good!" said Li Wo. "At what time, my brother?"

"She is fifteen," Fow Ming explained, "and it is high time that she should be married. But tell me, brother . . . will she be the only woman in this house? Will there be no mother-in-law to teach her wise ways?"

"If she is your daughter," answered Li Wo, "she has been well taught, and I have no fear for the future of her life with my son. Are we agreed in everything? But no. You should spend more days with me. You should see the boy again and again. It is not easy to judge so quickly."

"I have seen enough," said Fow Ming firmly. "And now, friend, since you are tired, I must leave you and go to bed."

So saying, he touched the cup of guest tea with the tips of his fingers. A steward came out with a double lantern on a bamboo stick to light the honored visitor to his chamber, and the host went with him.

At the chamber that had been assigned to him, Fow Ming went in with many a bow to his host, and the door was closed.

Then Li Wo went back into the garden. He stood in the dark of the poplars and willows along the water's edge, and called quietly. Instantly Ching Wo came from the trees and stood before him.

"It is ended?" asked Ching Wo.

The father raised one hand slowly above his head, an inexpressible gesture of triumph. "It is done!" he exclaimed. "It is done! The fool has walked into the trap, and he is entangled so completely that there never will be any escape for him. My dear boy, we shall sit up for a little while together and drink hot *samshu* and talk of the difference between fools and wise men."

V

A flare of wind made the nearest of the lanterns swing, and by the flash of light Li Wo saw in the face of Ching Wo pity, horror, and disgust. It brought the teeth of Li together with a *click*. He snapped his lean fingers so that they rattled together.

"What is the word in your mind?" he exclaimed. "Speak quickly! What evil word is on your lips to speak about your father?"

"There is no word," said the boy slowly, "but there is sorrow, sorrow, sorrow."

"And for what, boy?"

"He is your guest, and you will trick him. He is your friend, and you will shame him."

"The devils of the white men have entered you!" cried Li Wo. "You speak to your father as they speak

to theirs. They . . . the wolves . . . w'
eat the weak and the aged. This
Tzu of which you talked. This
you have learned."

"I do not mean to speak against
boy. "But I am sick in my heart."

"You are sick with hatred of your fat.
he does is abominable to you, and you s

Ching Wo was silent, whereupon
demanded angrily: "Say it quickly. It is true

The boy said in his quietly musical voice:
you, do I not hate myself?"

"These are mere words you have learned o
books. But what is the use of knowledge that ne
enters the heart? Your lips have become clever. Y
have learned to play a part to deceive me."

To this Ching Wo answered in the same subdued and
gentle fashion: "Is there one truth that our people
know? It is that the spirits of our ancestors guard us
and watch over us, if we give them honor. I am not
worthy, but I am not a fool and a dog."

Li Wo suddenly changed in his manner. Either his
heart had altered or else he was controlling himself
with care.

"Consider what I have done for you, Ching," he said.
"I am marrying you to the daughter of a rich man. You
will soon be surrounded by servants who do not need
to be paid with stolen money. There will be no more
raiding by night, and you can lead the life of an honest
man."

nest man?" the boy answered sadly. "Oh, m
hat honesty is there in such a life, which i
a lie?"

what lie?" asked Li Wo, controlling his temper.
have pretended to Fow Ming that you are a
ant."

m I not a merchant?" the other retorted hastily. "I
e my goods on sale. That is enough for the world
now about me and my work."

And how have you got the money to buy the goods
hich you sell?" asked the son.

"By the wits and the strong hand of my son," Li Wo
replied. "How could there be a better way?"

Ching Wo was again silent, and looked upon the
ground, with his hands thrust into the alternate sleeves.

At last he said: "And if Fow Ming should learn the
truth?"

"Of what use will the truth be to him, after he has let
you take his daughter?"

The boy sighed.

"And why do you sigh?" asked Li Wo.

"I have no wish to marry, Father."

"You are young," said Li Wo, "and you are a fool.
But you are old enough to know that I am wiser than
you. Therefore, you will do as I say."

"I hear whispers in the street behind me," the boy
commented. "There are people near us who have
wider eyes than you think. Someday they may find us
out."

"They never will find us out. As I have arranged this

matter, everything is perfect. You are free now to go to your bed. Tomorrow Fow Ming will return to San Francisco to prepare his daughter for the marriage. After that, she will be sent down to you."

The boy bowed, drew back a step, paused.

"Have you something else to say?"

"Yes. All the way down the river on the ship, I wished to speak to you, but I did not dare. In San Francisco I saw a list of people who are coming on the next ship. It will be there in a week, perhaps."

"How could such news have come?"

"It was brought in by the *Flying Cloud*, which sailed a few days after the other vessel. I read the list of names."

"What did you find there?"

Ching Wo hesitated. "I found there the name of our greatest enemy."

The father, puzzled for a moment, suddenly uttered a faint cry. And he stood before the boy with both hands extended, and his face twitching with a half-savage and a half-frightened eagerness. "What is the name?"

"Malcom Foster."

"Coming here? Coming into our hands, Ching Wo?"

The boy drew a breath. "If all the work I had to do were half as pleasant to me as the thought of finding Malcom Foster, the whole year would be April and May for me, if only. . . ."

"Ah?" said Li Wo.

"If only I could be sure."

"Of what thing, my son?"

"Oh, my father," declared the boy, "I should speak to you reverently, and, if my words are not pleasant, I should be silent."

"Nevertheless," said Li Wo, "speak freely and clearly for this moment, at least. What is troubling you?"

"You have often told me," Ching Wo explained, "that Captain Foster caused my mother's death. In all that you have taught me, you have kept his name in my mind. And if. . . ."

"Is it wrong that you should hate your mother's murderer?"

"You have told me other things, at other times . . . not of him . . . and often they have not proved to be true. When I first saw his name in the list and knew he was coming here, my heart leaped. I told myself that he was coming to death . . . my hand would hold the knife . . . I would kill him slowly and talk to him while he died. Thinking of that, I was happy. But then I remembered the other things you have spoken of, which have not been truth, and I have been sad and in doubt ever since."

As though the shock of this had almost unnerved him, Li Wo went a half pace backward, until his right hand touched the smooth trunk of a young poplar. Against this he braced himself, and the narrow head of the tree trembled.

"Am I a liar in the eyes of my son?" he gasped at Ching Wo.

The boy did not speak, but his face was contorted with pain. Great beads of sweat gleamed on his forehead.

Li Wo threw both his hands above his head. "If I have lied," he cried in a choking, almost sobbing voice, "may the sky open and a river of lightnings fall on my head! If he was not the murderer, and if my own eyes did not see the murder, may I be stricken to ashes! Oh, Ching Wo, Ching Wo," he added sadly, "it is true that I have spoken a great many evil things, and things that did not have truth in them. But it was he who forced me to it. It was he who made me a starving beggar, and forced me to steal. If I have done evil, it is his evil. It falls back upon his head. Ching Wo, now I shall swear. . . ."

But Ching Wo held up a hand in protest. Then he dropped upon his knees and begged forgiveness, whereupon Li grasped the hands of the kneeling boy and raised him up.

"You have committed a sin against your father," he said, "but if it were twenty times as great a sin, there still is blood enough in the body of Malcom Foster to wash it all away. It is not a murder. It is not even revenge. It is a sacrifice. The spirit of your mother will be made to smile. How can we tell? She may at this moment be standing in this garden listening to us, and pitying me because I have a son who cannot have faith in his father's word."

The boy, at this, threw a startled look around him, and a gleam of satisfaction appeared in the eyes of Li.

They parted at once, Ching returning to the house.

Li walked up and down through the garden. He was both worried and delighted. Worried by the questions that the boy had asked of him, and delighted that he had been able to parry and postpone the answers.

Sometimes he felt, when he dealt with young Ching Wo, that he was literally dealing with a thunderbolt that might well consume the wielder if he were not in the highest degree careful. But he felt, also, that he had acquired such skill in this task that he could continue it indefinitely.

So Li Wo laughed a little as he walked up and down in the dim light of the garden. He braced back his shoulders, and breathed more deeply as befits a man who has won a great battle.

At last he went into the house, but, before going to bed, he looked into his son's room, and found that Ching Wo was not there.

Alarmed, he searched through several rooms until at last he peeped into the chapel, where he beheld Ching Wo, face down upon the floor, with arms stretched beyond his head, so lost in supplication that he looked like one dead.

At this, the keen face of Li Wo flashed into the most evil of smiles. He let the curtain fall back softly over the incense-laden air of the chapel and over the wor-shipper. Then he withdrew to his own chamber.

More than once, as he was preparing for sleep, the father interrupted himself with musings and with a noiseless laughter. Toward the end, something troubled him sufficiently to make him get up and take from a silver box a quantity of slips of thin yellow paper, punched full of holes and covered with inscriptions.

He opened the window, and, as a breeze was blowing up the river, he loosed the paper from his hand and watched it go off like a thick flight of birds.

This bit of sacrifice to the evil ones being accomplished, Li Wo lingered at the window for a moment, listening to the far-off sounds of celebration from the dance halls of Buffalo Flat. Then he went back to bed, and fell at once into a sound, sweet sleep, untroubled by any dream of good or of evil.

VI

Fow Ming and Li Wo departed the next morning for San Francisco. They were to inform the bride of her approaching wedding and to make all of the arrangements. At the last moment, the bridegroom would be wanted and should appear. In the meantime he was at liberty.

Ching Wo accompanied his father and Fow Ming down to the boat, as in duty bound, and saw them aboard. He waited by the dock until the steamer had gone off, her stern paddle wheel flashing in a great arc behind her. Then Ching Wo turned away and mingled with the crowd.

Hardly had he done so when Sheriff Lefty Wilson approached him through the jostling people and laid a hand on his arm.

"I want you, chink," said the sheriff.

Ching Wo looked upon him with an innocent surprise. "Wantee me?"

"I want you," repeated the sheriff. "You come along, kid, an' don't you make no fuss."

A hale and red-faced merchant of Buffalo Flat had overheard the words of the arrest, and now he tapped the sheriff's shoulder.

"You're makin' a mistake, Lefty," he said.

"What kind of mistake?" demanded the sheriff, who was a man of firmly fixed purpose.

"I'll tell you what kind. This kid is the son of Li Wo. There ain't a straighter chink in the world than Li, an' the kid never has made no trouble in the world."

"All right," answered the sheriff, "then I'd like to know why he's usin' Handsome Harry Delancey's diamond stickpin to fasten up the neck of his shirt there?"

There was a gasp of surprise from the merchant. "It ain't possible."

Ain't it?" inquired the sheriff. "Once I had occasion to look at all of Harry underneath his mask, in particular that pin. I reckoned that I might need to know the face of it some other day, an' dog-gone me if I wasn't right."

Wilson laughed loudly as he said this.

"Well," said the merchant, "he might've bought it from somebody, you know. He might've bought it an' thought no harm."

"All right," said the sheriff. "I ain't sayin' that he's the blood-brother of Handsome Harry, am I? I just want to find out who he got that pin from."

It was a good diamond, of the purest water, and large in size. Brilliantly it flashed upon the black-shifted bosom of the boy, who looked down at it with a sort of innocent wonder, while he was carried off by the sheriff.

No crowd formed about them. A "damn' chink" was not worth even a momentary consideration. And so they crossed to the jail, and in the sheriff's own office that gentleman sat down with his prisoner.

"What's your name?"

"Ching Wo."

"Ching, where you get that pin?"

"My father, he give me."

"What for he give you, Ching? You talk up straight to me, an' it'll be the better for you. You may've heard that I'm the Chinaman's friend. An' I live up to the word. Yaller or white or black . . . the color of a skin don't make no difference to me. Wherefrom you get that pin, Ching Wo?"

"My father, Li Wo, he give me."

"What for he give it to you, Ching? Because of what he give it to you?"

"Me tlenty-two year old," said Ching, and smiled with pride as he said it.

"He give you a pin with a diamond in it like that for a birthday present, did he? Why dog-gone my hide if I thought Li Wo had the money to dash off things like that. It don't hardly sound nacheral at all to me. Ching, where'd he get the pin?"

"Not understand," said Ching Wo.

"The devil you don't," answered Lefty Wilson, who had the eye of a hunter of beasts and men. "The devil you don't understand. The fact is, you know all about it. You know the shop he bought it from, and the man that sold it to him."

Ching Wo stared blankly.

"Look here, Ching." said the sheriff, "I aim to take a fancy to you. You're too young to do no harm. You ain't the kind of chink that makes any trouble. I know the whole gang on your side of the town, an' them that wears knives, an' all of the rest. But I reckon you ain't that kind. I've always had a good report about you. You mind your business . . . you keep your face shut . . . they say you're gonna be a great Chinese scholar one of these days. Well, maybe you are, an' I hope you will be. But it ain't gonna hurt your chances to tell me the truth about that pin. Understand?"

Ching Wo looked in a frightened, puzzled manner at the ceiling, and then back at the face of the sheriff, very earnestly.

"Ching Wo tly understand." he replied in a soft voice.

The sheriff stood up. "You ain't gonna talk, then?"

"Ching not understand. Ching want to talk allee same," said the boy, trembling.

"Now, by God," thundered the sheriff, "you hit out with the truth, or into the jail you go, even if you gotta rot there!"

The eyes of Ching grew wider and wider until it seemed that his very soul could be seen through such capacious windows. But even though his lips parted not a word came forth.

The sheriff paused. He was obviously worried, and suddenly he shouted loudly: "Pete!"

"Hey?" grumbled a voice from the next room.

"Pete, come in here."

Pete Greggains came, big, red-faced, and red-haired.

"Pete," explained the sheriff, "y'understand how I told you about spottin' Handsome Harry's diamond pin? Now, here I've seen it on this here yaller monkey. He says he don't know nothin', he ain't seen nothin', and that his pa give it to him for a birthday present. What'd you do about it?"

Pete grinned with evil intention. "I'd take a couple of yards of blacksnake an' tie it around his neck. By the time you untangled him from it, maybe he'd remember somethin' else."

"Aye," said the sheriff sourly. "That'd be your way, but it ain't mine."

He was a tall, lean, bony man, was Lefty Wilson, with a prominent Adam's apple that wavered up and down his wrinkled, sun-tanned throat when he talked. It wavered now, as he regarded the boy.

Ching Wo seemed to have understood enough of this conversation to make him shrink back against the wall, and there he looked from one to the other of the white men. He clasped his hands together, not in supplication, but in utter terror.

"Aw, I dunno," Pete muttered.

He strode up to Ching Wo, and towered above him,

and then took the breast of the shirt in his large grasp and looked at the pin.

"It's a hummer," he said. "I dunno. Why not soak the chink into jail until his pa comes back from Frisco? It won't cost you nothin', an' you might work somethin' out of him."

The sheriff hesitated. "Well, I guess you're right. I hate to do it. I'd 'most rather to kick a dog than this here poor kid, because his skin is yaller."

"They say that he ain't so simple as he looks," said Pete.

At this both he and the sheriff looked firmly upon the prisoner. The wide, empty, frightened eyes of the boy turned from one to the other, as though he were trying to read his death sentence in a completely foreign language.

The sheriff spat upon the floor. "I guess I gotta do it. If it was any trail besides that of Handsome Harry, I wouldn't bother none. Search him, Pete, an' stick him into a decent cell, will you? I sorta hate this here business, damn me if I don't. But Handsome Harry . . . I'd like to know what shop he's sellin' his jewelry to. Why, Pete, if you come right down to it, it means somethin' that Harry is sellin' his jewelry at all."

"It does mean somethin'," agreed the jailer. "I'll handle the kid easy enough."

With this he fanned the boy. That is to say, he passed his hands over the body of Ching Wo, pressing the fingers carefully around the hips and beneath the armpits, the usual places in which weapons were carried in those days of the primitive, early West.

The jailer announced almost instantly: "He ain't got a thing. Only the pin."

"Take it an' put it in the drawer of my desk," said the sheriff. "Then shove the kid into a cell, an' come back an' join me. I got something else to talk about, out here in front. I'll be sittin' on the steps. The sun ain't too hot this time of day."

Pete removed the pin. Then he took from the wall a set of strong new handcuffs that fitted over the round wrists of Ching Wo. After he had secured the prisoner in this fashion, Pete led him into the cell room and showed him into a steel-barred cell. The door of this he slammed with a heavy clangor.

"There ain't anybody else around to keep you company, kid," he said. "But you'll be all right when your dad comes back . . . if he's willin' to talk a little. Take it easy. Don't you worry none."

But Ching Wo had thrown himself face downward on the soiled coverlet of the cot and did not raise his head to answer.

VII

No sooner was his jailer gone than the young Chinaman came to life in quick and stealthy fashion.

First he lifted his head and stared quietly about to make sure the cell room was, indeed, empty. Then he stood up from his cot, slipped off one of his soft shoes, and lifted an inner sole.

Beneath this there lay several tiny splinters of steel, which Ching Wo fingered for an instant, and selected one of them. With this in his hand he went to the steel door of his cell, and there, with a single easy movement, wriggled his hands out of the steel cuffs.

That left him free to work on the lock. Reaching beneath it, he raised a hand on the inner side and began to probe the mechanism.

This was a matter of utmost delicacy. With strained attention and bent head, Ching seemed entranced by distant music. Presently the bolt turned with a loud *click*, and the door fell open.

Ching stepped through into the aisle of the cell room, and for a moment waited there, listening intently. He heard someone laugh before the jail door, and recognized the sheriff's voice. Then a wagon rumbled down the street with a *jingling* of chains, a *creaking* of hubs and singletrees.

Reassured by this, the youth went swiftly on to the door of the sheriff's office. This was locked, of course, but the same splinter of strong and supple steel worked here, also.

Ching opened the door with practiced caution, pushing it stealthily, inch by inch, feeling every stir of it, and ready to move it as softly as the minute hand of a watch, for fear it should *creak*.

Thus the wily young prisoner managed it without a sound and stepped lightly into the room.

He went to the desk, first of all. The drawer was not locked, and from it he picked the diamond pin that had just been taken from him. Next, from a holster that hung on the wall, he obtained a good single-action Colt, which he dropped into his clothes.

Still he was not done. Sitting down at the desk, Ching took up a piece of writing paper and a pen, and wrote in a fine, bold hand as follows:

Dear Lefty:

You ought to confine your attention to me, and not bother my friends. You've frightened poor Ching Wo almost to death, and he's ready to run out of the country. So, of course, I took him out of jail.

He told you the truth. I myself gave his father the diamond pin to celebrate the kid's birthday. He's a decent young Chinaman, and was very good to me on several occasions, without knowing my name from Adam's.

Now, Lefty, I've taken the boy away, but I want you to notice that I've gathered in nothing but the diamond pin and a gun. I saw in your drawer—which you ought to keep locked—four good gold watches, some more jewelry, and a money pouch crammed with gold dust. I could have taken all of this stuff, and it would have been a good deal of a blow to your pocketbook and your reputation. But I preferred to leave it behind me, and I hope you'll look on this as a sufficient ransom for Ching Wo.

That poor boy means no harm, and he's actually afraid to leave the jail with me. However, I know what happens to Chinamen in this part of the world. I think you'll agree that they rarely have a fair deal.

Lefty, you and I have always played a man's game with each other. If you continue to pick on Ching Wo, I'll give a little time to some of your own friends. But I hope that this won't be necessary.

Always with kind personal regards, and the best of luck to you, I remain, Your obedient and humble servant,

Harry Delancey

P.S. By the way, you're quite wrong about that Morgantown affair. I'm not a wholesale cut-throat, like Murrieta.

Ching folded the paper and secured it with a pin, the head of which was a delicate specimen of that feather work that the Aztec Indians once had made into a fine art. It was the semblance of a tiny hawk not an inch long, and made with movable wings, head, and legs.

With a few deft touches he spread the wings, stretched forth the head of the little image, and tucked up its feet so that it seemed in full flight.

After he had done this, the youth looked about, to make sure that he had forgotten nothing. Then he left the place, locked the door behind him with a deft manipulation of the steel splinter, and crossed the cell room to the rear door. Here he paused, bent over the lock again, and for the third time he was able to walk freely through.

Shrugging his supple shoulders, the prisoner went quietly out, with no more noise than the drifting of a cloud shadow across the back yards of the white man's part of Buffalo Flat. Those yards were heaped with rubbish of all sorts, broken boxes, discarded cans, a veritable tangle of wrecked wagons and saddlery, and all manner of articles such as an improvident people will discard as soon as it is in the slightest degree difficult to use.

Moving in this manner, he successfully crossed almost half of the town unnoticed, keeping to alleys, yards, and byways, and so he came to the slough that divided the white from the Oriental section.

He did not risk crossing the humpbacked bridge, but found a boat moored against one shore and rowed in this to the other.

Five minutes later Ching Wo was at the house of his father.

In his own room, he lifted a narrow section of the floor and took from it a small bundle. This he examined with care.

It consisted of a sombrero hat, boots and spurs, a gay-colored waistcoat, a crimson scarf made of finest lace, which had all the look of a rich altar cloth, trousers trimmed not with silver conchos, but with burnished medallions of gold, and a short Mexican jacket set off with golden braid.

Ching Wo now added to his equipment a good rifle,

and a pair of his own guns, in exchange for the one that had chaperoned him from the jail.

He took, also, what appeared to be a single short-bladed knife, but as he picked it up, the weapon dissolved in his hand into six parts. It looked, when fitted into a single sheath, like one haft, but in reality the single semblance made six weapons. Not of the slightest use for hand-to-hand fighting, of course, but perfect to be flicked from the flat of the palm.

He picked up a few more odds and ends, then closed his bundle.

After this the youth touched a gong, informed a servant that he was going to resume his studies in the abode of his uncle, and straightway left the house.

He went down the riverbank not more than a quarter of a mile, kicked away the surface earth, and so turned up a cord that ran from a buried peg down into the water. He pulled up the peg and drew strongly on the water end of the rope.

Presently a dark shadow detached itself from the muddy bottom and came wavering up to the surface. There it was upended, and proved to be a very small and shallow skiff made of tin, so treated that it could not rust through the paint that covered it. Two oars were lashed along its sides.

After waiting for the water to drain out, Ching Wo entered the boat, placed his bundle at his feet, and, crouching in the narrow bottom, began to ply the oars.

The light craft slid like a water insect over the surface. Ching Wo, dipping the oars silently, shot the boat in long pulses down the shadow of the bank until he came to a small creek that entered the main river. Up the mouth of this he pulled a scant furlong, grounded the skiff, and stepped out with his bundle.

Then he went into the copse where the woods were thick. There he paused and lowered the bundle.

From his clothes he took out a small wooden tablet covered with Chinese characters. This he placed on the bundle and suddenly he sat down upon his heels, stretched out his arms, and raised his handsome, melancholy face to the brightness of the sky above him.

The singsong of the Chinese speech became music as he murmured softly: "Fathers of Li Wo, be close to me, in order that you may see my heart is clean, although now I am about to do again the thing which is forbidden. I am about to wear the clothes which are a sin, and speak the language which stains the mouth. But if I live like a hawk in the sky, you know for what reason, and how the white men treat all my people like dogs at their feet. Intercede for me for my sins, pure and undying spirits."

VIII

After he had finished speaking, Ching Wo remained for a moment, silently, in the same position, his eyes closed, his mind still working.

At last he rose with a sigh, stripped off the light silken garments he was wearing, and stepped into the outfit he had brought with him. The very shadows of the forest flashed with his new splendor. The bundle of discarded clothes he hid in a fork of a tree, then he walked on through the wood.

As he strode along, Ching lost the peculiar shuffling gait of a Chinaman and stepped out more freely. So he came out of the woods by the river into the open, and saw before him a little cabin with a tin smokestack leaning above it at a crazy angle. Behind were a small cattle shed and a straw stack of the year before, with a top blackened by winter rains. In front of the house stretched a few acres of vegetables and maize.

An aged Negro was harnessing an ancient mule to the plow and preparing to run a few furrows; he sang in a quavering, husky voice as he worked.

The Negro was not aware of Ching Wo's presence until the shadow of the latter's Spanish sombrero fell across his feet. Then he turned by degrees, as very old men do, his head moving no faster than his body.

"Good morning, Jim," said the boy.

"Lord, Lord a'mighty!" exclaimed the Negro. "Here's Mistah Delancey come again. I might've knowed you'd be here soon for the gray hoss. I knowed it all the time!"

"And yet you've turned him out to pasture again, you old rascal?" asked Ching Wo, with a good-natured smile.

"He might be out at pasture," said the Negro, "an' he might not. I ain't sayin', 'cause I dunno."

"You don't know?"

"I ain't a bird in the sky that could look fifty mile' aroun' an' see. I dunno where the gray hoss is, boss. Three ge'men come by in a mighty hurry, an' one of 'em had a lame hoss an' he changed saddles onto El Rey, an' off they went."

Ching Wo folded his arms with a gesture that might have been recognized as the thrusting of hands into invisible silken sleeves.

"What did they look like, Jim?"

"They was two Mexicans an' a white ge'man with bowlegs an' a powerful big look about him, an' red hair. He done changed his saddle onto El Rey, an' he says, says he . . . 'Him that leaves out a hoss of this here kind, he's too big a fool to deserve to own him.' Then they rode on off up over the hills yonder."

The boy considered with a calm face and a quiet eye. "I'll take the pinto and follow. Did you change that off fore shoe on El Rey?"

"Done change it yestiday, Mistah Delancey. I guess you gonna have no more use for Uncle Jim since I los' your hoss for you, Mistah Delancey?"

But Ching Wo merely waved a graceful hand. "How long ago?"

"More'n two hours, boss. An' two hours of hosses such as they was ridin' would mean fifteen mile', anyway."

In the shed Ching Wo found a tough pinto mustang, on the back of which he cinched his own saddle. Then he rode off, with his Winchester in the saddle holster and a small pack behind the saddle.

The boy proceeded at a steady canter, never pressing his horse, but swinging it steadily on, while he alternately scanned the roadway, where the new print of hoofs appeared, and then the nearest skylines.

He had not gone a mile when the trail left the road and stretched away across the open country, and now he found more difficulty. For the trio were making a strong effort to cloud their trail.

On a broad space of gravel and rock, where the marks of the hoofs practically disappeared, they had doubled back. Half a mile away they returned to their former course until they reached a creek. Here the trail disappeared in the water and did not climb out on the farther bank, but, at the very first long cast up the stream, Ching Wo came upon the sign again, not a quarter of a mile away.

After this, the three seemed to be satisfied that they had constructed enough trail problems to block all pursuit, for they went on boldly, keeping to the southeast.

For whatever point they were bound, they were pressing hard for it, as though anxious to keep an appointment. Ching Wo, with skillful eye, could tell that the three horses were weary, by the shortening of their stride at the gallop. Presently it became the long, rolling lope of the true Western cow pony.

The gallop of El Rey was a different matter, and lucky was the man who sat in the saddle upon that glorious horse!

Months before, when Ching had first stepped into the white man's rôle—for which Li Wo had trained him with such care, and over so many long years—it had been a serious difficulty to the youth of Oriental culture. But now he began to feel that when he put on the clothes that made him into Handsome Harry Delancey, he was transforming his heart and soul as well. He could almost laugh aloud at what was sacred to him in the garb of Ching Wo, the young Chinese student.

So he began to gladden his heart with the beauty of the day, without trouble in mind.

For it was such a day as only California can show. The sun was keen and hot, but in every shadow was a refreshing coolness, and across the hills ran a rich riot of wild flowers. He saw a whole hillside winking with golden buttercups, and beyond, in the horizon mist, the poppies flared like a sheet of flame.

Shortly after midday he made a halt to refresh the mustang and complete his own disguise.

This he did by taking off his hat and allowing the queue to fall forward over his shoulder. From the end of it he then untangled the threads of black silk that prolonged the pigtail, and his natural hair he worked into two very flat braids, encircling the head.

Next, from his pack, he took out a black wig and brushed it out with the greatest care. This he fitted into place, and at once there was lost to his face the half blank and the half whimsical expression that most Chinamen derive from the height of their shaven foreheads. Instead, he now had long black curls that swept down from beneath the brim of his hat and gave him a dashing cavalier look.

That done, Ching mounted again and rode on through the warm afternoon. The pinto gradually became sweat-blackened and powdered with dust. His canter shortened. His head drooped. But still he worked honestly until the sun floated like a crimson bubble on a western hill behind them, and, coming to the top of a slope, Ching Wo saw that the three riders before him had turned into the brush beside the road.

IX

Ching Wo, alias Handsome Harry, dropped out of the saddle and, kneeling at the roadside, examined the hoof prints in the roadside grass. For a moment he could learn nothing. At length he made sure that several of the blades that had been trampled were stirring, raising themselves a little toward their normal erect position.

By that the youth knew that the trio had passed this way only a few minutes before, and he looked keenly about to plan his next line of action.

To one side was a higher hill, more sparsely covered with bushes. Up this the Chinaman determined to go for a commanding viewpoint over the countryside. This was hazardous work, for, if he were spotted, Ching had no doubt that they would pick him off with their rifles. However, hazards he was accustomed to endure, and he sent the weary but game little mustang laboring up the hill.

Twisting this way and that, knocking up stifling

clouds of dust as they grazed brambles and shrubs, they soon were at the summit, and from this the young man surveyed a surprising panorama. At the very first glance he reined the mustang violently back, dismounted, and then crawled along on hands and knees.

He could look out, now, from a nest of rocks that crowned the hill, and he saw two things of the utmost interest.

In the first place, at the rear of a low hill just beneath him, Ching could see three horses distinctly, only half sheltered by the brush since he was looking down at such an angle, and among the three he noticed the silver back of El Rey.

In the second place, at the front of the hill, where it looked upon the road, he observed two men sitting behind a screen of bushes, and presently he saw a third—there were rifles in the hands of each.

Then, to complete the picture, he discerned in the distance six horses that came nodding over the top of a hill, tugging a coach behind them. Presently the horses were trotting, then cantering as they swept down into the hollow beneath.

They disappeared, and only a plume of dust smoked up out of the depression in which they were lost to view, but the boy had seen enough. He who sees a crouching tiger and an ox grazing nearby is not hard put to imagine why the tiger is in wait.

Ching Wo, from his hilltop, laughed until his white teeth flashed. Then he climbed back on the mustang and took a headlong course down the same slope up which he had come. His plan was clear.

He circled close under the foot of the hill and came straight up to the spot where the three horses were tethered. All were big, handsome animals, but two of them were badly spent. Only El Rey seemed perfectly fit.

The reason for the hard riding was not difficult to find. Here was a point that the stage would reach just at sunset time; the brush skirted the road closely and was sufficiently thick; moreover, this was a spot from which the robbers quickly could escape into the back country.

Ching Wo, taking note of this, gathered the lead ropes of the horses and mounted the gray. The stirrups were too long for him, and he could judge by this that a very big man had been riding El Rey. But the good steed knew his master, and, in spite of the great distance he had covered during this day, he now went easily.

In swift cavalcade the horses were taken to the side of the higher hill, where Ching Wo dismounted and examined his catch. These were no impoverished robbers. And certainly no religious scruples bothered them. For out of the first saddlebag that he opened, Ching Wo took a chamois bag containing a rosary with a golden cross and beads of ebony wonderfully chased with gold, and in the same bag was a quantity of cheaper jewelry.

Ching Wo wrinkled his nose. He was not a believer in Christian divinities.

From the second bag he took out only two things. One was a silver button from the top of a Chinaman's cap. The other was a rawhide thong, the ends of which were much twisted around and around as though a stick had been turned in them. He looked attentively at this strip of leather and rubbed from it two or three tiny pale shreds; here and there the thong was stained dark.

Ching Wo's face turned demoniacal. For he could visualize the scene with wonderful clearness: the Chinaman—a man of rank, to judge by the button of his cap—cornered by the ruffians, forced upon his knees, the secret storage place of his wealth demanded of him, and, when he refused, the thong bound about his head, the stick twisted. . . .

Men said in the house of Li Wo that they had seen their compatriots endure this torture until the eyes burst from their heads. Some had died under the slow pressure.

Ching Wo, lifting his contorted face, cried out through his teeth: "Kuang Ta, let me be the man to kill him! May he go through all of the ten regions of hell! May he burn for thousands of years, and be transformed into a blind worm at the end of his punishment!"

Ching trembled with fury, and he searched no more through the saddlebags. It was enough for him that he had found a thing that, in his eyes, condemned all the three men to a horrible death.

Guns *crackled* at that moment from the other side of the hill, and he ran El Rey to the rear shoulder to see what had happened on the road. It was the kind of picture that had been viewed before by Ching Wo. He nodded with familiar appreciation.

One masked man stood at the heads of the horses, his rifle covering the driver and the guard, who apparently had made no effort to use his sawed-off shotgun. A second man, similarly masked, kept his rifle trained on the passengers. The third, pistol in hand, stood by to superintend the rifling of the boot.

A mailbag was thrown down from it. Two trunks followed, which the third robber knocked open and looked through the contents. After he had finished this, the passengers were lined up in a row—six men and a woman, with the driver and the guard. Their hands stiffly held above their heads, they waited while two guns covered them, and the third masked bandit went through their pockets.

When the rifling of the party had been completed, one of the passengers was withdrawn from the others, and his hands tied behind his back. With this he was taken back into the brush by the fellow armed only with a revolver.

Instantly there was confusion. The woman ran forward, but was struck by one of the ruffians and staggered back.

Ching Wo's face tingled as though he himself had received the blow. It was a thing he hardly could believe, for usually he had seen the white men treating their women almost as though they were honorable, divine ancestors, rather than workaday flesh and blood.

The remaining pair of bandits—one carrying a sack of loot and the other a canvas containing the guns of the men of the stage—now disappeared into the brush.

At once the passengers pooled together in the wildest excitement. Out of that confused group, the woman broke suddenly and ran headlong into the bushes.

The others wavered, then in a solid charge they rushed forward behind her. Dust puffed up from the shrubbery in the rosy light of sunset. A single gun barked, and out from the brush recoiled the seven men of the stage, one of them supported by two of his comrades.

Ching Wo, seeing this, smiled again, with his white teeth glinting. After all, they had been fools to venture into that entanglement without weapons, and they had had their reward.

But the woman did not return.

The rest of the people hesitated only an instant, and then poured into the stage. None of the traces had been cut, or a wheel damaged, as often was done when stage robbers wished to isolate their victims for a long time.

Apparently the three desired only that the stage would get out of the district as quickly as possible, and now they had their will, for the coach was presently at full speed down the road, the horses galloping hard and the driver using the long lash of the whip. They were going for help.

Ching Wo thought of the rage and confusion in the

first town they would reach, with the news that a stage had been held up, a man abducted from it, and a woman lost in the wilderness.

A woman lost!

Ching laughed at the thought. For were not women, of all of God's creatures, the cheapest and the least useful, except that a man's mother was necessarily a sacred ancestor?

However, the youth saw that the time had come for him to act, and straightway he put himself in motion. He had intended to take only the three horses, but the discovery of the bloodstained rawhide thong and the Chinese button had changed his mind completely. When the three reached the spot where they had left the horses, he intended that bullets should meet them.

So Ching Wo sent El Rey sweeping across the hollow like the swooping hawk that was his most loved emblem.

X

When he came to the place where he had found the horses, Ching dismounted and threw the reins of the gray stallion in a place where the thicket closed around him.

Then the boy crouched by the edge of the clearing and listened, his ear to the ground. Voices came from a little distance higher up the hill, and they were not approaching. A moment more and he heard the woman cry out in horror or fear.

It stabbed the very brain of Ching Wo to hear that cry. And suddenly he was working his way forward through the brush, swiftly and subtly as a snake. He had left his rifle behind in the saddle holster, for he knew that for such close work as this the two revolvers were infinitely better.

The voices grew louder as Ching approached. He could hear the woman weeping. And a shrill, high-pitched man's voice protesting with a savage energy.

So Ching Wo came to the edge of the place, and crouched panther-like behind a bush through whose branches he could see fairly well into the group before him.

They were all here. The three masked men stood with two of them watching over the bound prisoner, and a third with his grip on the woman's arm. Her head was bowed; she was weeping into her hands.

Ching Wo sneered in disgust. All white women were like this—noise makers, trouble makers, running into the fire in the secure conviction that their men would rush forward to save them from harm.

The man who had been dragged from the coach was in the later middle age, with hair already silvery, a transparently thin and pale face, and shoulders bowed a little as if by ill health or long leaning over a desk. He had a nervous way, which Ching Wo did not respect. Nevertheless, the Chinese youth felt that the white man was intelligent and honest.

He was talking angrily to the woman: "Margery, what under heaven made you follow me? What good could you do, except to ruin me by putting yourself in their hands?"

"I didn't think," replied a stifled voice, choked and sobbing. "I only knew . . . I was afraid for you, Father."

Ching Wo jerked up his head suddenly. His head touched the branch of the bush just above him and rustled the leaves.

"What's that?" inquired one of the highwaymen.

"Snake sneakin' off," said another. "You shut up your yappin', Linton, an' let us know what we wanna know."

"And what d'you want to know?" asked Linton crisply.

Young Ching Wo heard these words only dimly. He was staring at the bowed figure of the girl with bewilderment and dismay, for she had expressed something that every Chinaman must respect, a filial piety stronger than the fear of death.

So he stared at her, lying rigid with wonder.

From his infancy, Li Wo had carefully informed him of the vices of the white man, his drunkenness, his foulness of mouth, his murders, his cruelty, his savage and incredible rapacity. In the picture all was crimson and shadow, but now it was subtly altered, for the mind of Ching, by a golden light.

One jewel there was in the heap of stones, one tender and faithful soul among all the treacherous. Her tears became, to Ching Wo, sanctified. A fragrance, as it were, breathed from her like the fragrance of the candles that burned forever before the god of his father.

Ching closed his eyes. He looked again, and yet this thing was not a dream.

The largest of the robbers, he with the tuft of red at the back of his head, now answered the prisoner.

"Linton, we know why you're goin' up to the hills. But what we wanna know is where?"

The prisoner jerked up his head a little. And suddenly he laughed. "I'm going for my health, of course."

A brief silence followed this. Then the red-headed leader strode closer and towered above the captive, who repaid him with fearless glance for glance.

"You got nerve, I see," said the robber. "I never doubted that, but don't be a fool. Five month back you come inta San Salvadore clean outta your head with fever, an' in your pack was a chunk of ore that looked rich enough to pay about a million a minute. Now, Linton, you're headed back for the same district, an' you're gonna stake out your claim. It's a good idea, but you ain't gonna get there. We aim to stake that little ol' claim an' work it for you, an' drink your health in red-eye night an' mornin'. We want the location!"

"And you expect me to tell you?" asked Linton, with a curl of his lip.

Ching Wo nodded. He could sympathize with such a spirit as this. He even began to guess that this man might be the worthy father of such a daughter.

"Gonna get yourself tapped on the head, are you?" growled the other. "Are you as big a fool as that?"

"I'm as big a fool as that," said Linton quietly. "That discovery nearly cost me my life. It's stolen ten years away from me, I imagine. You think that I'll talk for fear of a gun?"

"*Aw*, not a gun," snarled the leader. "They's other ways of makin' you talk."

He chuckled with a brutish complacency.

"I know what you mean," Linton responded. "I know your methods. Well, my friend, you can try them all. You'll soon see whether a slow death means any more to me than a quick one."

"*Bah!*" said the leader.

The girl raised her face suddenly. It was streaked with tears, red with weeping, but all that Ching Wo saw was the blue of her eyes and the yellow gold of her hair. Those things slipped like the grace of heaven into his soul.

He stared, and could not believe, and stared again. Ching thought of the round faces and the slant eyes of the Chinese maidens he had seen—and his blood was iced. Was his mother such as they, she who he worshiped? And the daughter of Fow Ming, too, who was to be his bride?

The youth closed his eyes and his pulse raced. Then he heard: "Don't be a fool, chief. This here is the same kind as that gent in Monterey that. . . ."

"Shut up!" bellowed the chief. "What were you gonna say, you jackass?" Then he added fiercely: "They ain't only one of 'em. We got two here. You understand that, Linton? It ain't only you that we're talkin' about? Seems to me that they's a pair!"

Linton stared at the speaker, then turned sharply and looked at the girl.

She herself had grown white, but she said rapidly, in a trembling voice: "They don't mean it. They wouldn't touch me. Don't even think about me. They. . . ."

"Won't we?" sneered the other. Then he laughed, and his laughter rumbled heavily upon the brain of Ching Wo, making his hand close hard upon the revolver he held.

Linton shrank a little. The young woman was white as stone, but she managed to shake her head, to stammer something, as though to say she was not afraid and she need not be considered.

But Linton said hoarsely: "I'll tell you, then. It lies. . . ."

But Ching Wo had heard enough. He, too, would have been glad, ordinarily, to learn where a rich strike was located, but this affair was different. An air of sacredness lay upon Linton, because of his daughter; therefore, all of his belongings, all of his affairs, must be preserved from injury.

The Chinaman, still in the rôle of Handsome Harry Delancey, rose from behind the bush at this moment and saw the eyes of the girl flare wide with incredulous joy and wonder.

His first shot was not for the leader—Ching would regret that afterward—but it split the heart of him who grasped the arm of Margery Linton, so that he lurched forward with a face grinning from agony and shock, and fell to the ground.

The red-headed leader whirled. "Delancey!" he groaned, and struck with the gun that hung in his hand.

The blow missed the head of Ching Wo. It was not for nothing that he had spent the long hours of wrestling, learning to read the motions of an enemy by the shadows that pass across his eye.

And as the big man lurched forward, Ching pulled the trigger to end the fight, with the muzzle pressed against the robber's side.

The hammer dropped with a lifeless *click* upon a dead cap, and the red-headed leader plunged on, the brush closing in a green wave behind his back.

XI

The second revolver whipped into the left hand of Ching Wo as he whirled after the big chief. From the left hand he sent a bullet splitting the brush in the wake of the robber. But the crashing sounds continued without a stop, and there was neither curse nor shout to indicate the bullet had struck home.

Another shot *cracked* behind the Chinaman, and a slug *hissed* close to his cheek. So he turned again, only in time to see the brush beating here and there. The third of the trio, having missed his revengeful shot, fled through the dusk.

The sky was one vast sweep of crimson and purple, and in the west were golden towers breathing out light, but still, beneath the shrubs and trees, the shadows were turning to smoke that darkened every moment.

At such a time Ching knew he could not have handled both his enemies. Had there been only one, he would have followed through the shrubbery as eagerly as ever a ferret followed a rabbit. But while he was handling one, might not the other return to the girl and her father?

What then? He would sooner have left the gods of his household exposed.

So Ching Wo, turning to the girl and Linton, touched the cords that wrapped his wrists and instantly his hands were free.

"Can you shoot?" he asked, offering a revolver.

"Not with a pistol. I can handle a rifle fairly well," Linton answered in the most matter-of-fact manner.

The elderly man picked up a fallen rifle as he spoke, and his daughter, with an air half-frightened and half-resolute, followed that example.

Ching Wo, who had seized on the sack of loot taken from the stage, now said: "Follow me in single file. Step where I step, and listen as we go. They may close in and try to take us from each side."

Then he went rapidly down the hill, nervous, but unwilling to go so fast that the others could not follow. He feared lest one of the fugitives might have cut in to where he had left El Rey in waiting, and that loss he would have regretted deeply.

So they left the dead robber lying where he fell, face downward in his mask, and Ching Wo glided before the Lintons until they came to the screen of shrubs.

The guide half expected that guns would spit fire at

him as he approached, but he was wrong. The red-headed man was not there, and El Rey stood with his brave eyes glistening in the dusk.

Ching mounted at once, because from the saddle he could see more clearly across the brush on every side. The darkness was increasing so rapidly now that it was as though a shadow were rising from the earth.

Thus the youth known as Handsome Harry led the way forward until they rounded the side of that steep hill that had served him as an observation tower to such good purpose. There they found the other horses still waiting.

"Here are the mounts they were riding when they stopped the coach," remarked Ching Wo. "Take your choice."

"By the way," said Linton, "Margery, this is Mister Harry Delancey."

She acknowledged the introduction with shining eyes.

Ching Wo, remembering his rôle, dragged off his hat and bowed deeply.

"I'll have something else to say to you, Delancey, if you'll walk aside with me," said the elderly man. Then he spoke to his daughter over his shoulder: "Stay here a moment, Margery. I want to have Delancey alone for the moment. Don't worry. We're not twenty miles from San Salvadore, and, if Delancey will rent these horses to me, we can make the trip easily."

In the meantime he and Ching Wo stood facing each other beneath a tree.

"Delancey," he said, "you've got me out of a mighty bad tangle just now. I want to talk gratitude. But not merely in words. Let us see what you'll get out of this." He paused.

Ching Wo smiled a little and waited.

"You'll get what the thugs took from the stage," went on Linton. "No matter what it is, you deserve it. And by the weight of it, and the number of wallets and watches, I judge it to be worthwhile. On the other hand, that's your just booty, and doesn't have anything to do with your services to me and my daughter."

"Are you going to pay me for that?" asked Ching Wo.

Linton shrugged his shoulders, as though to banish from his mind the suggestion of cool contempt in the voice of the adventurer.

"Let's be practical," continued Linton, "and not sentimental fools. I'm a rich man. You want riches. Now, then, Delancey, I have a checkbook in my pocket. I want to know, simply, what you'll have me write on the check?"

Ching Wo was silent.

Come, come," said Linton dryly. "Suppose I offer you five thousand? You can cash it for face value in San Francisco at my banker's. Very well, then, you take five thousand now, and, after I get to the mines, if you come into trouble or need of any sort, you'll be free to drop in on me and make a call for, say, a similar amount. What about it, eh?"

He talked like a businessman putting his proposition half coldly, and half in the tone of conviction of a man who is not driving a hard bargain and knows it very well.

Ching Wo merely smiled again.

There was still some glow in the sky, and he was facing west, so that sufficient of this glow came upon his face for Linton to observe it. The mine owner was checked in the midst of his argument by something mysterious, by something of another world, or another race, he could not tell what.

As a matter of fact, he could have seen a similar expression come many a time upon the face of any Chinaman, wrapped in meditation, divorcing his thoughts from the earth, flying into the dreamy and bright obscurity of the Buddhistic ideal.

But Linton had no thought of such a thing. "You won't have it? Not enough?"

"Mister Linton," said Ching Wo, "you are kind. You speak to the point. I understand exactly how you feel about this matter, and that you don't wish to be under obligation to a ruffian."

He had stepped back swiftly into his character of Handsome Harry, and Linton responded with a grumble.

"Look here, Delancey, I haven't called you such names, so don't put them into my mouth. I don't want to be penurious. I'll double the offer, if that suits you. If not, tell me what you want to do?"

"I want to get onto my horse," answered Ching Wo, "and I want to ride with you. I'll take you into San Salvadore."

"Very well. Though we're perfectly safe."

"If you scare off a pair of hawks from the chicken yard," said Ching Wo, "they're sure to come back. You're not safe alone. Shall we start?"

XII

Ching Wo rode first, for, as he pointed out, it would be useless to pool all of their party in one body, which might be riddled at the first volley of ambushers.

Keeping 100 yards or so in the lead, he passed through the section of the road where the trees and shrubbery made dense walls of shadow. As they came out into the open country beyond, where the way dipped only now and then through dark clumps of trees, Ching drew back once more to the side of his companions.

This he did with much perturbation of spirit, for it seemed to Ching Wo that his very soul was in peril on this day.

Foreigners were devils. Of that the youth was sure, because his father had taught him so with sacred authority since his boyhood, and he could not doubt the lessons of Li Wo. Nevertheless, every moment across his mind was running the picture of Margery Linton as she had started into the shrubbery after her father. What strength had she to help him with her weaponless hands? But she had gone blindly ahead, drawn by her duty.

This thought stung the heart of Ching Wo with

wonder and joy. So he told himself a dozen times that he must remain in the lead, beyond earshot of them, and yet, as the road grew clearer, he found himself dropping back.

The moon cast a strange illumination over the white road and made the trees like great, wavering shadows beside it. By this partial light, Ching watched Linton and, covertly, the girl, also.

Margery's head was constantly half turned toward him, listening and watching, and, although the upper part of her face was lost under the shadow of her hat, from nose to throat Ching could see her, and the smile upon her lips.

There was no doubt that the young woman was very happy, and from the manner in which she continually watched him, Ching Wo wondered if he did not form part of her pleasure. Or was it only Margery's joy because her father had been released?

"Delancey!" Linton spoke abruptly. "I want to talk to you."

"Certainly," said Ching Wo, turning to the man beside him.

The Chinese youth found he could look steadily into the lean, grim face without that thrill of disgust that he usually felt when confronting a white man. And this astonished him. It gave him a little pang of fear and remorse. He could not decide how to explain this adventure to Li Wo.

"Delancey, how long have you been following this life?"

"What life, if you please?"

"This gadding about the roads . . . this living at the point of a gun?"

"Why," considered Ching Wo, "I've been doing this for about . . . well, say fifteen or twenty thousand miles."

Linton chuckled, enjoying the manner in which his question had been answered and parried at the same instant.

"What do you get out of it, my lad? We all expect some return on our investments of time and trouble, saying nothing of our safety."

Here the girl turned her head more decidedly toward Ching Wo, and her smile vanished.

"Why," said Ching Wo, "you see that I'm a traveler, and the fifteen or twenty thousand miles I've ridden have been their own reward."

"Because of the scenery?" asked Linton dryly.

"Exactly." Ching Wo beamed. "If a man looks in the right way, he'll find almost anything along the road. Every now and then I find a patch of gold dust flowers that only need to be picked and shaken into a money belt."

"You might be called a maker of honey, then, Delancey?"

"Thank you," responded the boy. "It's never been said in just that way, but I suppose it is wild honey."

At this, Linton and his daughter laughed in unison, but suddenly they heard the rapid *thrumming* of hoofs on the road behind them.

They were at this moment climbing the side of a steep hill, and, looking back over the brow of the hill to the rear, they saw half a dozen riders sweep around the curve and flash into view, like so many ghosts in the dim moonshine.

"Who are they?" gasped the girl.

"They're hunters," said Ching Wo. "And I think that they're running in sight of the quarry. Listen. They're giving tongue."

As they listened, they heard the exultant whooping of the six riders as they rushed their horses down the intervening hollow.

XIII

Instantly the three had their horses at a gallop. Ching Wo, ranging between the Lintons, considered the gaits of the animals and told himself that they were too tired to last very long. El Rey, of course, sustained his strength, because there was in the stallion an inexhaustible well of power, and even when his limbs began to fail him, he could run ten miles on his mighty heart alone.

He called to them loudly: "Push straight ahead! Don't race your mounts, because they can't stand it, but keep them at a steady gait. I'm going to fall back and try to make the road a little rougher for the men behind."

The girl turned toward him and cried out something. Ching did not understand the words, but thought he made out something about "sacrifice". The youth took off his hat and waved it back, the long black hair of his wig blowing back over his shoulders. Then he swerved El Rey about and swept into the trees at the side of the road.

It was a noble forest of yellow and sugar pines, and behind a giant of the former kind, with its bark cracked in a huge pattern, he brought the gray stallion to a pause. Then he pulled the rifle from its long holster beneath his leg.

The woods were both lofty and open. The moon shone down through the irregular foliage of the evergreens, making a pale silver pattern that glistened on the bed of pine needles. A small stream crossed the road from the upper hillside at this point, and Ching Wo listened to its faint melody while the receding hoofs beat softer in his ears and the approaching ones rang more loudly.

He could hear one man in a bull's voice calling out to his five companions to hold their fire until they were close up.

Then the six riders burst over the brow of the hill and rushed into the sights of his steady rifle.

It was merely a question of whom he would drop. One life, at least, lay in the palm of his hand, his for the pressure of a trigger, but the youth hesitated. For it seemed to Ching Wo that beside every one of these men rode ghosts of women, every woman young and beautiful like Margery Linton.

He gasped, with a new sort of fear in his heart, and

then picked out the leading rider—and fired low.

He saw horse and man lurch down, the rider with a wild *screech* like a cat suddenly struck by an eagle's talons. The horse did not stir where it fell, but the rider tumbled head over heels, lurched to his feet, and staggered blindly forward under the impetus.

As for the rest, they split aside from the road suddenly as water shunted from a slanting rock, and with a roar they had changed their direction, shouting curses.

Ching Wo heard only one word, the name: "Delancey!"

His white teeth flashed in the moonlight as he reined El Rey about. He liked this game. No matter how hard they rode, dodging among the mighty trunks of the pine forest, he would match El Rey against them.

Only five heads, now, and perhaps fewer later on.

A shadowy horseman raced through the trees not fifty yards away. Thrusting the rifle into its holster, already reloaded, Ching Wo snatched out a Colt and fired a bullet—this time at the fellow's head.

He knew he had missed even as he pulled the trigger, but the horseman, with a yell, bent low in the saddle and drove off down the slope.

That was the beginning of a strange battle in the pines, for Ching Wo ranged to and fro, gradually driven back, but still shooting at every human form he saw. Once he heard a shout of pain and rage in answer to such a bullet, and knew he had at least winged another of the group.

That made four remaining. Ching guessed that these would not press too close upon his heels!

He was right.

Presently there was no more sound of panting horses. They had given up their charging, then, and had taken to stalking tactics but, in the meantime, stalking took time, and the real prize was some distance away, on the road to San Salvadore.

A gun barked suddenly from the side of the next tree, not ten paces away, and Ching Wo heard a bullet whisk past his ear.

But he did not shrink. A burst of wild savagery took him by the throat, and, spinning El Rey about on his heels, he plunged straight at that tree.

A frightened shadow broke away from the safe shelter of that pine trunk—a man on foot, running with arms thrown out before him, like a child fleeing from some nightmare horror. As Ching Wo reached the fugitive with a single bound of El Rey, he covered the man's head with his Colt.

And then again a haunting mist blew coldly upon his brain—a new soul seemed to cry sadly in his ear. Taking his hand from the trigger, he spun the weapon about and struck down the fellow with a crushing blow across the head.

After that he went straight up to the road.

There were only three heads remaining on the dragon's body, and Ching felt a grim assurance that when they had counted their losses, they would ride no longer upon the trail this night. On the edge of the road he paused again. Behind, in the woods, he could hear voices coming faintly through the thin mountain air, and they were the voices of cursing and rage. So much for that.

Before him lay the moonlit way, surely empty of danger now, and leading straight on to San Salvadore. To Ching Wo it seemed that the road was leading still farther up a continual hill that was no harder to climb than is the hill of the blue heaven to a soaring hawk— and at the end of that road lay happiness. What it was he did not know, but it wore for him the smiling face of Margery Linton. The thought made his heart sing in his breast.

Laughing, he rode forward and, rounding the next curve, came fully upon Linton and his daughter.

Linton himself threw up his rifle to cover the approaching rider, but the girl knew better, and instantly dragged down the barrel of the weapon.

"You're not hurt, Delancey?" called out Linton anxiously.

"Not a scratch. But why didn't you go on and on?"

"I know that was your plan," said Linton, looking cautiously into the shadows of the trees, "but I couldn't keep on the road . . . when I heard the guns behind me. Where are they?"

"There are only three left," answered Ching, a sudden joy filling him because he had allowed a ghost to turn his aim. "And they won't worry us any more tonight."

But the girl did not speak. Wondering at this, Ching

looked so closely through the shadow covering her face that he could see tears passing, with a faint gleam, down her cheek.

XIV

On the outskirts of the town Ching Wo left the Lintons. San Salvadore was roaring like a storm wind, but an elderly man and a girl would be safe enough in that wind, Ching understood.

Moreover, it would be too sensational an entrance, riding the horses of the very men who had robbed the stage, and carrying into San Salvadore the loot that the robbers had taken. So he said good bye at the verge of the lights.

Margery Linton barely touched his hand, but her father gave a prolonged grip.

"Delancey," he said rapidly, as one almost ashamed of his emotion, "we've gone farther tonight than we've traveled in all the rest of our lives, and without you we never would have come to harbor. The property they would have stolen . . . why, that's a small thing. But as for the rest . . . I can't talk about it. But from this moment I hope you'll look on our home and whatever we have as your own. Good bye, Delancey."

Linton rode off with his daughter. She had not spoken, but unexpectedly she glanced back and brushed away a tear.

Ching Wo was satisfied. And, indeed, what words

could have compensated for that sudden, instinctive turning of her head?

He watched them out of sight down the winding street, and then set about his own affairs. As surely as hawks fly for prey, so Ching Wo journeyed under the guise of Delancey to pounce upon fat game. This very evening San Salvadore would be his hunting ground.

He had to look to El Rey, first of all. In a thicket near the waters of the creek he put the stallion. Then he ventured to a nearby livery stable and bought hay and crushed barley to give the gray a liberal feed.

Sometime before morning Ching Wo might need the full strength and speed of the big horse again. So he waited a moment, studying the breathing of El Rey and, with a few wisps of hay, rubbing the sweat from his body.

At last Ching was convinced that the big fellow would do well enough, so he left the thicket and boldly entered town.

Like many another mining hamlet, San Salvadore was strung out beside the windings of a creek. There was one main street, from which alleys and short crossways forked at irregular intervals.

Down the main street Ching Wo walked with a light step. Keen was his eye as he strolled along, whistling merrily.

Most of the people were wandering aimlessly, looking for fun and fighting, or merely bent on hearing the latest gossip. Some dropped in at the wide doors of dance halls, gambling saloons, and mere drinking bars, while from the same doors others came out.

In the crowd were miners, still wearing the heavy flannel undershirts in which they had worked all day. High-hatted gamblers were sauntering about to take their turn at a table, or looking for easy victims. There were dark-faced Mexicans, always in defensive groups of two or more, and tenderfeet newly arrived from the East, with a hungry and half-frightened look in their eyes.

But there was one overmastering tone in all of these people. The ground that had been cursed for Adam's son had given up raw gold, and every man there was dreaming of wealth. There was not a mind that was not partly in the world of fancy, sitting in shining coaches, or walking through the halls of great mansions.

Ching Wo, searching for his prey, studied faces and clothes. He had found one and then another promising victim. Suddenly he heard an accusing voice.

"I've got you now! That was a cold hand you lifted on me, you dirty cur. . . ."

Such words bring only one kind of rejoinder. The crowd melted swiftly back to either side from the path of danger, and Ching Wo saw a slender youngster shaking his fist in the face of a burly fellow with a brutal face and his neck cloth set off with a great diamond stud.

The latter seemed to be considering his denouncer thoughtfully for a moment. Then his hand jerked back and came into view again, bearing a shimmering Colt.

The boy, too, made a convulsive effort to get out his weapon, but he was slow—slow as death, it seemed to the expert eye of Ching Wo. A gun roared, and it was from the hand of the tall man.

Ching Wo saw the victim clutch his shoulder, where the bullet had torn through. It was not a death, but it was perhaps an arm ruined for life. And Ching, slipping back through the wave of incoming people, drifted after the victor.

The latter, without haste, but with long strides, was withdrawing from the hurly-burly, and now sauntered steadily up the street. Plainly he was a cautious man, and knew the rules of the game. There were such things as vigilante movements, and one never knew when these might start. So the gunman would withdraw to his own place and wait there until the excitement had died down.

Like a hawk steadying for the swoop, Ching Wo held on the trail. This was his victim for the day.

The big man, passing quietly down the street, came to a narrow and dark alley, where the slanting moonlight did not reach the street. Ching Wo, following, saw the gunman whirl about, at bay. From the hips up, moonlight bathed the fellow and shone upon his savage face. Dark shadow covered the rest of him.

"Who are you?" asked the stranger.

Ching laughed. "I'm a hawk."

"*Bah!*" came a sudden grunt of disgust. "You're a drunk, and a fool!"

"I'm a hawk," persisted Ching. "A wild hawk looking for easy meat."

"You're a half-baked slice of nothin' at all," declared

the other, "an', if you trail me another step . . . get back onto the main street or I'll bash your face in."

The bully came with his left hand poised heavily, and his right hand ready for the draw that might be necessary, but Ching Wo leaned against the wall and laughed, with the moonlight on his face.

"A hawk, a hawk," he said. "And there's a sign to put on you, my friend, like this."

Something in his voice, in the clear enunciation of his words, seemed to warn the big man of danger. At any rate, he paused abruptly in his advance and made again that lightning movement of the hand.

It had been more than fast enough before, but now it was ages late. With one unbroken movement, the long Colt slid into the hand of Ching Wo and continued in an outward flash until it was dashed into the face of the other. The long barrel *clanged* against the skull of the gunman, and he sank in a drunken stagger.

The arms of Ching Wo received him, laid him gently on the ground, and the hand of Ching Wo slipped a stuffed wallet from his coat, the diamond from his scarf, and the gold watch from his waistcoat pocket. Then, with the touch of a knife, the money belt strapped about his waist, next to the skin, was clipped in two and dropped into the pocket of the boy.

Still Ching was not done, for he took out another of those little gems of feather work that represented a gray hawk, and arranged this with upward slanting wings and forward-stretched feet, like a stooping hawk about to strike. This he fastened into the crown of the stranger's fallen hat.

Then he stood up and dusted his hands and knees. Still a trifle worried, he bent once more and laid his hand upon the heart of the stunned man.

That heart beat steadily, regularly.

"What the hell is this?" growled a voice behind him, as a pair of men turned into the alley mouth.

"Poor fellow's drunk as a lord," said Ching Wo calmly, stepping back from his victim. "He's fallen on his face and cracked his head. You'd better get him home if he's a friend of yours."

The youth was moving backward all this time. At length he stepped around the corner and slipped into the next group of men that moved in the main street crowd, as he heard a voice shout from the alley.

"It's Doc Peters! He wasn't drunk five minutes ago. . . . Hey, where's that smooth-talkin' kid?"

But the "smooth-talkin' kid" was already lost in the heart of the crowd, walking with a light step and a cheerful whistle still upon his lips. He had the flushed face of one who has just come from the gaming tables a winner.

Thus he went on through the street, regardless of shouting and confusion that had grown up behind him. Apparently the friends of Doc Peters were making some disturbance.

But the disturbance did not come near him, and soon Ching sat on his heels beside the feeding gray stallion and counted in his hands $1,700, besides sundry incidentals.

XV

Sheriff Wilson was entertaining in his office the other political power of Buffalo Flat. This was the mayor of the town, Fatty Rourke.

Rourke's office did not bring a large salary, but he found other ways to build up a pleasant income. His labors consisted in warm handshaking, bright smiles, and many speeches. He had a gay strain for weddings and a solemn strain for burials, and he could touch many strings in between.

As for the sheriff, he had to run upon his record in office and his notable courage. His record had been excellent up to the moment Harry Delancey rescued his prisoner, Ching Wo. The liberation of a Chinese was not very important, but it had caused several thousand men and women to laugh at Lefty Wilson.

So Lefty had sent for the mayor and asked for his advice, as an expert politician.

Said Fatty Rourke: "Give 'em time. They'll come around to you, Lefty. They ain't any doubt about that."

"Ain't there?" growled the sheriff. "Man, the election is short of a month away, an' Porson says he's gonna run. It wouldn't be easy to beat Porson, no matter how many scalps I had at my belt. Gents don't throw votes for you when they're laughin' at you, Fatty, an' you ought to know it."

"Take things easy," insisted the mayor. "This here chink that's got away . . . he don't amount to nothin'."

"Sure he don't. It's Handsome Harry that makes all the hell for me."

"Delancey's slick," agreed Rourke, "but you ain't the first man he's dodged around."

Wilson nodded.

"Bud Hall was found dead in the woods, halfway between here and San Salvadore. Likely it's more of Harry's work."

"But Hall was one of Red Phil Saunders's gang," said the mayor. "I dunno that they's any need to cry over that kind of spilt milk."

"Maybe not," said Lefty.

At this there was a knock upon the door, and it was pushed open before the sheriff had time to answer.

The jailer appeared in the opening, an odd expression on his face. "They's a chink here wants to see you, Lefty."

"Damn all the chinks in the world," said the sheriff bitterly.

"This chink is by name of Ching Wo, an' I figgered. . . ."

The sheriff nodded, whereupon the silk-clad form of Ching Wo, slender and shrinking, entered. He looked paler than ever. His eyes, opened very wide with fear, were fixed upon the face of Sheriff Wilson.

The sheriff, in the meantime, had risen slowly from behind his desk.

"Ching Wo," he said.

The boy shuddered.

"Ching Wo, what in hell am I gonna do with a jail-breakin' chink like you?"

Ching's lips parted, but no words came. He stood as one regarding a nightmare.

"The kid's scared to death," said the mayor. "Give him a chance, Lefty."

"You sneakin' lyin', yaller-skinned monkey," growled Wilson. "What brought you back?"

Ching Wo again attempted to speak, and finally gasped: "Ching Wo flaid!"

"Is he?" The mayor grinned. "I never seen a chink much more paralyzed than this one."

"Maybe he is," Lefty agreed, "but if he's scared now, he's gonna clean pass out before I'm finished with him. I'm gonna make this here kid a damn' fine example. I'm gonna skin him, an' tan the hide, an' cover a dog-gone' saddle with the pelt. That's what I'm gonna do."

This he said with appropriate gestures, coming halfway across the floor and acting as though he were about to rip the poor boy in two the next instant.

Ching Wo raised one arm and put it across his face to ward off a possible blow, and cringed lower against the wall.

"Hey, Lefty," the mayor interceded, "listen to me, will you?"

"Well, what is it?"

Still glaring at the young Chinaman, the sheriff allowed himself to be drawn into an opposite corner of the room.

"Look here, Lefty, is this here chink important?"

"Him? Not a bit, except. . . ."

"Not a bit is right. Suppose you raise hell with the kid, what good is that gonna do you? People will say you're lettin' the big guns get away with murder, while you take it out on the little ones. Here comes a scared chink, an' gives himself up after he's been set free. Well, that's a feather in your cap. You hurt Ching Wo, an' the boys will call you a bully. But you treat Ching Wo white, if you take my advice."

"Feed him on chicken an' cream, eh?" retorted the sarcastic sheriff. "Make him at home in the jail, you mean to say."

"I'd never take him back into the jail at all," said Fatty Rourke.

Lefty elevated his eyebrows.

"You wouldn't what?"

The mayor's smile beamed.

"I'd turn him loose. I'd let him go, an' tell everybody that what you want is the bull, an' not the calf. That'll make a hit. The boys will all see that you're a man's man, an' that's what they want for sheriff in this here county."

This bit of political diplomacy was a long reach above the head of Lefty Wilson. He could only blink.

"All right," continued the mayor. "I've said my say. You do as you please, but, mind you, they's a couple of thousand votes for you in this if you handle it like I say."

"You think so?" muttered Wilson.

"I know it. It's a grand play for you."

The sheriff sighed, still with hungry eyes fixed upon the boy. But then, as though suddenly seeing the light, he grinned broadly.

"I see what you mean," he said. "Maybe you're right. Besides, I got nothin' ag'in' the young chink. He's always been a quiet citizen as far as I know. No opium, no gamblin', no nothin'. Well. . . ."

He strode up to Ching Wo.

"Listen to me, Ching," he blustered. "I oughta take an' chuck you into a jail an' keep you there for life. I'd oughta half starve you in a dark cell. But you're young, an' I reckon Handsome Harry made you go along with him. All right, kid, you get out, vamoose, get along, an', if I ever hear of you an' Handsome Harry Delancey again in the same breath, I'm gonna hang you up by the ears an' leave you to dry in the sun. Now, get. You savvy?"

Ching Wo listened with an amazed face. Suddenly he broke into a profusion of very low bows, and so, with murmurs of joy and gratitude, he backed out of the room.

He went out onto the street and passed down it slowly, pausing for a moment at the corners, and sometimes looking behind him. At length he turned about, for he had seen Mayor Rourke coming rapidly toward him.

A moment later they rubbed elbows in the crowd. Neither spoke. Each looked blankly and fixedly straight before him, but suddenly the good mayor felt a solid little weight chug home into his coat pocket, and a smile creased his cheerful face.

He knew very well what was in the package. It was a pile of beautiful, freshly minted $10 gold pieces, twenty-five in number, and he could tell himself that he was doubly paid—by the gold of the Chinaman for the good he had done him, and, afterward, surely by the gratitude of the sheriff for such good advice.

Nothing could be better business than this. A certain sense of joy that was almost virtue swelled the mayor's heart. Every person who passed him on that street nodded to himself and was glad that the political fortunes of Buffalo Flat were committed to the hands of so worthy a man.

XVI

Ching Wo went home, and there, having passed through the outer rooms which, during all of these years had served as so effectual a blind to the police of the white man's town, he entered the real house of Li Wo.

The first thing he saw was, in the shrine room where the Buddha stayed, just below the image itself, a big card lined with red paper. On the outside was the image of a phoenix; inside, two needles, strung with silken thread, were stuck fast.

He knew well what it meant. It was the Chinese betrothal card, now drinking the same incense smoke that went in the service of the Buddha itself, and more sacred and binding upon a Chinaman than a Christian marriage actually completed, oaths and all.

Ching Wo, looking upon this, felt his skin prickle. Chills slid like serpents down his back.

He examined the card well, and found it contained a long and honorable list of the girl's ancestors, as in duty bound it should.

Then, unable to remain longer in front of the thing, he muttered rapidly a few prayers to the Buddha, feeling sick at heart.

After that the youth went in search of Li Wo and found him in the garden, seated in the full strength of the sun. Li's head was bared, and his yellow face wrinkled with a smile of contentment.

Ching fell upon his knees and greeted his father.

Li Wo bade him rise.

"I have completed everything," he said, "and it is all well. I have seen the girl, Yen Ming, with my own eyes, and found her simple and virtuous. She is graceful as a lotus flower, and fragrant as wild honey."

The boy's heart shrank, for he remembered the words that he himself had spoken on the night before, when he had ridden down the road toward San Salvadore. Wild honey. It brought before him the face of Margery Linton, the very sound of whose voice stirred through his mind like far-off music.

He lowered his eyes, murmuring: "I am glad."

"You are not very glad," said his father dryly. "However, you will be glad later. But you have been away?"

"I have been away."

"Then where?"

"El Rey was stolen from the old Negro who keeps him. I followed him to San Salvadore."

Suddenly Ching felt it would be much better if he said nothing about the two Lintons.

"And there?"

"I found the horse. Also, I found a man carrying more money than he needed. He was not a good man . . . he was a bully and a gambler. . . ."

"Listen to the boy," said the father almost fiercely. "You talk of good and of bad as though every white man were not devoted to the devil! But go on . . . what did you do?"

"I took his wallet, his money belt, and his diamond."

He laid them, article by article, on the lap of his father as he spoke.

"There were two hundred and fifty dollars more. I gave them to the mayor, because he made my peace for me with the sheriff. You know that I have been in his hands since I left you?"

"I know," said Li Wo. His eyes burned as he looked at the boy. "I thought it was the end, and that from this moment you would have to live like a hunted rabbit. But is your peace really made?"

"Yes. I paid the mayor money . . . I went and trembled before the sheriff. That was all."

He sneered a little as he spoke, and Li Wo laughed while he counted the money and weighed the gold dust.

"There is enough here for your marriage . . . more

than enough," said Li. "We can feast a hundred for ten days on this, if we choose. But we will not choose. Filled bellies are for pigs, and not for men, as I have often told you. A lean dog is a quick wit. Ching, you came from his trail without being recognized?"

"Yes. The little sign of the hawk, my father, is all I left behind me."

At this the father stretched out both hands and brought them together, clenched as fists. Great was his exultation.

"For ten thousand blows and curses and revilings and robberies which they have inflicted upon our people, you will repay them with your life, my son." Li was greatly excited. His breast heaved rapidly. "Ching, you carry with you the tablet of your mother?"

"Always," said the boy.

"You say prayers to it every day?"

"Every day of my life."

"I have told you that a white man caused her death, my son. Now I am going to tell you the whole story. Sit down."

Ching had been hoping and dreading to hear this for these many years. As he slipped down upon his knees, his face was bloodless with anticipatory horror.

"We left Foo Chow together, your mother and I," said Li Wo. "We sailed on a fast ship out of the Min River and headed across the great sea for Hawaii. And from the first the white men looked from the corners of their eyes at me, because I sailed with them in the cabin, and not with the coolies in the hold of the ship.

However, I did not pay much attention to them, because already I knew that they were dogs, unclean swine, liars, untrue to their parents, and. . . ."

He paused, and waited until his emotion had subsided a little.

Then he went on: "Your birth was not due for another month, but this was how you came to be born. There had been a theft from the captain's cabin, and he, like a devil, accused me, and ordered me to give the thing back. I could not give it. It was a little string of pearls that belonged to his own wife, who was with him on board the ship. And she . . . do you hear, Ching Wo? She, also, was about to have a child!"

His excitement mastered him again, so that his lips worked violently.

"The ship's captain was Malcolm Foster, who I have often mentioned. When he accused me of the theft, and I told him truthfully that I did not have the pearls, he swore that he would beat them out of my skin. He triced me into the rigging and flogged me . . . with his own hands . . . like a dog . . . and I fainted under the strokes.

"Your mother came from our cabin and saw the whip fall on my naked back. She fell to the deck, and the next day you were born, as we came near to Honolulu harbor."

Li Wo raised his voice a little.

"Now listen and see how the gods first punished the brutal man. For, as you were taken from the side of your mother, and, as she sickened and asked for help

128

in the fever, I ran to the captain and begged him to send the ship's doctor to her. But he laughed. He struck me in the face and drove me away. His own wife, he said, was sick, and the doctor had to be with her.

"I sat by your mother's side and watched her grow mad with fever. I prayed to all our household gods. I even prayed that my son would die if my wife could live.

"But my prayer was not granted. The child lived. After a while I knew my wife was dying. I ran again to the captain and begged for help. I found him sitting with his head in his hands.

"Listen to me, Ching Wo, and you will see the power of the gods . . . how terribly they strike, and how quickly. The head of this man rested on his hands, and he was sick in his face, and white. For his wife had given birth to a male child, also, and that child was dead, was dead, was dead!"

Li Wo laughed horribly, rocking himself back and forth.

"At last the ship's doctor came, looked once at my wife, and said it was too late. I could only sit by her side and say to her many times, as she cried out in her delirium . . . 'Wei Sung, all is well, for our child is a boy. He is strong, and he smiles in his sleep.'

"So I sat by her until at last she made a small cry in the middle of the night, and thus she died."

Li Wo drew his robe over his head.

Ching wavered a little on his knees, but not with weakness. It was a fierce and overmastering passion that consumed him, made him tremble as a flame trembles, for he felt as though he had been walking the deck of that ship and had seen all that his father had told him, and that he had leaned over his own mother and watched her die.

At last, his face still half muffled and his head bent, Li Wo muttered: "Malcolm Foster, as you probably know, has already reached San Francisco, and already he has left it. He is traveling up country toward San Salvadore."

Ching leaped to his feet. "I shall go and meet him, then. I shall go and make him welcome to this country, my father."

Li Wo, fiercely contented in spite of his grief, said slowly: "Later, my son. But now your bride is coming to you. After the wedding you shall meet Captain Malcolm Foster."

XVII

When Fow Ming carried his daughter to meet her future husband, it was agreed that he would take her overland in a carriage especially hired for that occasion.

A mounted courier and guide went on ahead, and reached Buffalo Flat several hours before the carriage would arrive. He gave warning to the groom and the prospective father-in-law. Li Wo, being already prepared, sallied out to meet the welcome guests.

He was going several miles down the road from Buffalo Flat, on foot, in order to do greater honor to rich Fow Ming. In the meantime, Li enjoined his son, who had several bachelor hours remaining on his hands, to spend most of this interval in prayer for the happiness of the union, and for the purity and the virtue of his household.

But Ching Wo prayed for only ten minutes. Then he slipped from the house with a bundle under his arm, went down through the river trees, and drew from the water the same tin boat he had used before.

It was mid-morning. Under the bright hot sun, which turned the face of the river to thin steam, he shot the skiff down under the shadow of the bank and across to the other shore.

There the young man landed in just the place where he had arrived on his previous excursion, and there he changed his dress among the trees.

But on this occasion he made himself like a poor peon, with a straw sombrero on his head, and a greasy mustache, and the cheapest of blue jeans, and heavy, clumsy boots upon his feet. He decorated himself still more with a strip of narrow plaster that puckered the skin along one side of the face and gave him the appearance of one who had been wounded severely in a knife fight.

In a few minutes he had transformed himself into a dangerous-looking ruffian. The mildness of Ching Wo was shaken off with his silken garments, and a young brute stood in his skin.

He went on to the house and found the Negro chopping wood. The aged man paused, axe poised in air, and stared at the youngster.

"It's I, Uncle George," said the boy. "I've come for the pinto again."

"It's a mighty dog-gone' down-headed hoss, that pinto," responded Uncle George, "evah since you rode him out that day on the trail of Red Phil Saunders an' his men."

"*Hush!*" Ching warned. "Don't let even the trees hear you say that."

"Lord, Lord," ejaculated the old man, "I ain't even gonna think that name, then. I'll get yo' hoss for you,

"I'll get it myself, Uncle George," said the youth.

Presently he rode out of the barn with the pinto beneath his knees.

He traveled at a steady canter until he had put some distance behind him. In this manner he left the woods and emerged into a clearing where a small shack stood.

At the door he drew rein and called.

Two voices answered. Then two Mexicans came to the door and looked out. They stared at the horse; they stared at him.

He said to them in good Spanish: "It is I, my friends."

"You are yourself, perhaps," said the older man, knife-scarred as much, in fact, as Ching now appeared to be, "and you yourself may know your own name . . . but what is that to me?"

"You are José Pinal?"

"I am José Pinal."

"That is Ricardo Pinal?"

"That is Ricardo Pinal, to be sure."

"You are the men who held up the Los Banos stage last winter?"

They drew a little closer together and looked at him out of narrowed eyes. They said nothing, but ventured to exchange one expressive glance with one another.

"You are the friends, also, of Harry Delancey?" asked Ching Wo. And suddenly he laughed.

José Pinal uttered an exclamation and stepped closer, peering hard. "All the little devils! This is *Señor* Delancey, Ricardo, and we are two bats who cannot see when the sun shines. *Señor*, dismount, come into our house. I wish to God it were a palace for you. Come in. *Santa* María! I never see you without thanking God for the neck that you kept from being broken!"

"I cannot come in," answered Ching. "But if you have no great business for the next ten days or so, I can give you work."

"We have ten cows," said Ricardo frankly, "and they are better without us than they are with us."

"I'll pay you five dollars a day apiece. Take enough food to last you, but be quick. We need to ride hard. I know that you don't let your horses rest between steps."

They did not say a word. One of them ran for the horse corral and soon had caught up two horses and saddled them. By that time his brother had made up two small packs. And in ten minutes they were riding down the road at Ching's side. They asked no questions, but while they cantered on together, Ching told them briefly his plan.

Half a mile farther they found a ferry that quickly put them on the farther side of the river. Still they galloped on down the river road until they came to a forking of the way.

Here, in a grove of oaks, they halted at Ching Wo's direction, and waited.

It was not yet noon. The air was still, the sun very hot, the fields covered with shimmering waves of reflection like the dance of almost invisible flame. Not a horseman or a vehicle appeared on the way. They could hear the *cooing* of doves from the trees on a nearby slough. A steamer went swiftly down the river, trailing a great black cloak in the air behind it.

Then Ching Wo saw what he wanted. It consisted of a carriage such as was often hired out for private journeys in the days before railroads penetrated that section of California. Two men were on the front seat. One, even at a distance, was seen to possess the queue of a Chinaman.

"They are coming," said Ching Wo.

At this, Ricardo and his brother put over their heads great masks, which were black draperies of cloth with ample eyeholes, and secured beneath the chin with strings so that the blowing of the cloth might not impede vision.

They uncased their rifles, also, and crouched at

watch, while the carriage rolled closer, its two horses kicking up a single cloud of dust that sagged away slowly to the south. The body of the carriage was covered with an iron-braced shade, from the sides of which thin curtains hung, but the stirring of the curtains revealed two people inside.

The carriage reached the forking of the road, slowed, and turned to follow the river way to Buffalo Flat. At that moment Ching Wo stepped out before the heads of the horses with a leveled revolver in either hand.

The battle ended that instant without a blow.

It was a half-breed Mexican who drove the horses, a man with a fierce face that suddenly turned yellow with fear. He rolled from his seat and dropped like a log to the roadside. The Chinaman beside him, although his own face contorted with pale terror, actually gripped the rifle that leaned beside him, but he thought better of it, and jerked his hands above his head.

In the meantime, there was a wild outburst of Chinese chattering from the carriage. Ricardo Pinal had taken from the carriage a slender girl, veiled heavily from head to foot, tottering so slowly on her pathetic little bound feet that Ricardo lost patience. Picking her up in his arms, Ricardo tore off the veil and carried her bodily away.

After her loomed the formidable figure of Fow Ming. He leaped from the carriage and jammed his breast right against the muzzle of the rifle of José Pinal, demanding the girl. Then, suddenly controlling himself, he said, in fairly good Spanish: "My friends, I am not a poor man. Give me back the maiden. I will pay you well for her. What is she worth to you?"

"Stay over there back by the carriage," said José Pinal. "*¡Amigo!*" he called to Ching. "Search the other pair!"

Ching searched them. He got a mere handful of silver from the pair, but Fow Ming yielded a great harvest. Two pockets were crammed with his wallet and his purse, and both were filled. Then he was made to reënter the carriage. Enter it he would, but he was in such a state of fury that Ching stepped close to him and said: "She will be as safe as if she were in your house, and after a time she will come back to you. Make your heart easy. And . . . collect your money to buy her again."

Ching could have laughed as he thought of the irony of this.

Then, ordering the carriage to be turned, he sent it *clattering* up the road at a brisk trot.

XVIII

The plan of Ching Wo was very simple. He and José Pinal returned at once by the same ferry over which they had crossed, leading the horse of Ricardo Pinal. He himself was to wait until night, and then row across the river in a boat that his brother would bring over. Fow Ming's daughter would then be kept in the house of the Pinals and well treated, but carefully watched as long as it was the pleasure of Ching Wo.

There was only one difficulty or danger, and this was for the boy to return to his house before his father, disappointed and waiting on the road, should go back to Buffalo Flat and the house on the river. For that reason, with José Pinal he made good time back to the ferry, found it about to start, and immediately embarked.

The ferryman regarded them with a sour eye. He was an ex-sailor, with one wooden leg and a formidable bulldog pipe forever clutched between his teeth.

The pair paid no attention to him, but, as they disembarked, José Pinal cast a single ugly glance. "That old fool sees too much and thinks too much. Well, who cares? I suppose the Chinaman will pay a big ransom for the girl, *amigo?*"

The Mexican grinned.

"Whatever he pays," said Ching, "we split into three parts. But keep her safely, and don't frighten her. If you do, she may jump in the river and take herself off your hands. He will hunt for that girl with men and dogs and money. And if he finds her at your house, you're apt to have your throats cut."

Ching spurred the pinto into the river woods, and rode rapidly back to the place of Uncle George. With the old Negro he left the pinto, then hurried on to the place where he had hidden the tin skiff.

A few moments later, once more it was the silken clad Chinese boy who sent the boat skimming across the river to the farther shore, sank it by the bank, and presently sauntered into the house of his father.

He came with a blank face, but with every nerve tingling as he passed the ancient gardener and felt the eyes of the old man trail after him and make a tremor in the small of his back.

There were suspicions about him among the servants of the house, Ching Wo well knew. His frequent absences could not be taken for granted by a people as cunning and wily as these. And all of his careful modesty, gentleness, and obedience, which he was forever showing in the house, and his long hours of study when he was at home, were now serving only to excite their suspicions the more.

Ching Wo went straight to the shrine.

For the very soul of the boy was tormented with misery and self-doubt. To him the most sacred of earthly things was his father. It hardly mattered that he knew Li Wo to be a rogue, a thief, and often a hypocrite. That father he had disobeyed and secretly thwarted, for which disobedience all of the household gods might forever curse him.

So Ching prayed prostrate before the grinning face of the Buddha, but he found that prayer was hard, for the smile of Margery Linton formed in the candle smoke and dissolved, and formed again, and left him trembling half with joy and half with superstitious dread.

Then he felt eyes behind him. Rising, he saw Li Wo at the entrance curtains, with the dust of the road on his finest clothes, and his face puckered with rage. The father demanded: "Where have you been?"

"I have been out on the river," Ching answered.

"And why on the river?"

"It was the last day when I could sit on the river and dream of marriage, Father."

"Sit and dream? Sit and dream," said the father. "Where would you have been if I had come back before this with your wife?"

"I should have heard you on the river road, Father, and it would have been easy for me to come back here before you."

The whole face of Li Wo withered with suspicion. But he spoke not another word on the subject. He had said enough already to make Ching's soul a thing of lead.

"Shall I go into the garden?" asked Ching. "Is it there you have left them?"

"I have left them in the dust of the road!" Li Wo snarled bitterly. "I have left them in the heat and the light of the road."

Ching thought it best merely to gape at this.

"All the devils slide into the bodies of Mexicans," said Li Wo fervidly. "May they die as they live . . . may they blow away like dust . . . may they feel fire in their veins, instead of blood!"

"Mexicans?" inquired Ching Wo in a troubled voice.

"You fool," said Li Wo, "why do you stand there and gape like a baby? You have horses and you have some knowledge. Go at once! Three Mexicans have stopped the carriage of Fow Ming and stolen his daughter to hold her for ransom. Why are you standing here? Go, go!"

He added, as the boy bowed and turned: "No. It's much too late for that. It would take days and days. And when you found her, you might find her dead. No, that is the care of Fow Ming. He who prides himself on looking like a warrior . . . he, the hero . . . he the great man, the rich man. He could not keep her safely, and now let him pay for it. There are other girls in San Francisco. I shall find you another, and we shall not wait for the daughter of a fool, no matter how rich he may be."

His fury as he denounced Fow Ming quite overmastered him, so that Li Wo had to walk up and down for a moment. Then he said: "It is time to be calm, quiet, and thoughtful. I have great things to tell you. Go into the garden and let tea be brought there. No, let it be wine. I shall come out to you at once."

Ching Wo was very glad to have this terrible interview ended. Hastily he went to the garden and had hot *samshu* brought in little covered cups, and a stock of it in a covered pot.

When Li Wo came, they sat down on mats and sipped the pungent liquor.

It was late afternoon. The sun began to pour slanting golden streams through the trees along the riverbank and the river mist was burning like a pale golden fire. Li Wo sat facing that sun, his eyes squinted against it, so that he had a most evil look.

Then he said: "The man who flogged your father and murdered your mother is to be this night at Slater's Crossing. He expects to go farther, but two of his horses will turn very sick this afternoon, and he will stop at Slater's Crossing." The Chinaman laughed viciously. "What do you propose to do?"

"I?" asked Ching Wo, his eyes opening in surprise. "I shall meet him tonight in the hotel at Slater's Crossing, and surely he will be dead before morning."

Li Wo continued earnestly: "With Captain Foster are five men. They are going with him to the mines, and every man is a chosen fighter, every man has sailed under him as their captain. The Americans fight as though they love death. Suppose you find them all sleeping in one room?"

There was a moment's pause.

"This captain is a snake," said the boy calmly. "Who would be ashamed of stealing on a snake and cutting off its head while it slept?"

A smile of singular brightness appeared upon the face of Li Wo. "Go, then. All the spirits of your ancestors wish you well. Oh, Ching, we have lost a good Chinese wife for you, but, if the murderer is killed, I shall find you the finest daughter of a Mandarin."

XIX

Slater's Crossing was not eight miles back from the river on the road to San Salvadore, and Ching Wo reached it in the dusk of the day after a slow and easy ride. There was no need for speed now, and El Rey might well require all his strength before the morning came.

Moreover, the rider desired a slow gait to match with his own meditations, for his mind was full.

He had seen suspicion glint from the eyes of his father, and the sight had not been pleasant.

Well he knew that no Chinaman's soul can hope for happiness hereafter unless he passes into his moment of death filled with reverence for all his ancestors—above all, for his father and mother.

Upon the thought of that mother he never had seen, he had poured out his heart, as a boy knows how to do, and worshiped her, and made an image of her in his mind, beautiful, and with his own pale skin. For she had possessed that same pallor, Li Wo often had told him, coming as she did from the north, where there are tribes almost as white-skinned as the Caucasians.

It was a clear-eyed youth who rode into Slater's Crossing that evening, and in the stable bought oats and hay for his horse. The horse itself he left in some woods at the rear of the hotel, for it well might be that he would need to leave the place so quickly that he could not wait in the stable until his mount had been brought out and saddled by a sleepy groom.

His action elicited no comment. For one thing, the hotel was crowded with people on the way to and from San Salvadore, and the stable was fairly filled.

The hotel was the cheapest sort of frame shack. Voices could be heard from one end of it to the other, but it counted fifty beds in some fifteen rooms, which sometimes were put side-by-side. That was not the limit of its accommodation, for often travelers were glad to make down their bunks in rows in the barn-like dining room, and even in the kitchen, paying 50¢ a head for the privilege.

It was a typical overflow night at Slater's when Ching arrived, after providing for his horse. He found the verandah filled with men who already had eaten their supper; the second table was now full. The bar was jammed and barkeepers were liberally pinching out gold dust to pay for the drinks.

Ching was reasonably sure that the people of Slater's Crossing did not know him, but he could not tell what travelers might have seen Handsome Harry Delancey.

In that name was half his pride. In that name he rejoiced with a peculiar malice, because it meant that he had met the white man in his own field and been accepted upon a certain, high plane. He was considered a dandy, an exquisite. He—Ching Wo!

His white teeth flashed in the darkness of the verandah as he listened to the fragments of talk about him.

Suddenly a chorus of thundering voices broke out in a chant, attracting many of the hotel's patrons to the spot from which it emanated. Ching went with them, for he had smelled the salt sea in that ballad, and from the salt sea came Captain Malcolm Foster.

"Who's up there?" he asked the man next to him.

"I dunno who. I can't see with my ears," was the rough answer, but a fellow behind them spoke up.

"That's Foster's sailors. They figger to make a pretty clean-up at the mines."

Loud laughter and cheering followed the next song, when the window of the corner room, next to that from which the uproar proceeded, was jerked up with a *slam*, and a gruff voice exclaimed: "Belay that, you shellbacks! Belay that, and turn in. The next watch will be on deck before morning. Turn in and shut up, the lot of you!"

The sailors instantly were silent, and even the listeners muttered rather respectfully.

"That's the skipper, Cap'n Foster. He's a flyer, too, they say. He's come out in ninety-three days. . . ."

"That's a lie!"

"It ain't. I. . . ."

But Ching strolled away. He had learned what he wanted to know—the location of the room of Captain Malcolm Foster. He could not help wondering if the worthy skipper would turn out with that watch that was to appear before the morning.

XX

What Ching had seen at the window was a pair of burly shoulders and a short, dark, square-trimmed beard. He was glad of that picture of the man, for it fitted perfectly into his idea of the brute who had flogged his father and caused the death of his mother.

He sauntered slowly down the verandah, still listening, until a name caught and stopped him.

"Doc Peters?"

"He's heading back for San Salvadore."

"Never knew that crook had left it. He always made the cards be good to him."

"Sure, he's been personally introduced to all the aces, Doc Peters has . . . but a while ago he skinned out of San Salvadore like a wildcat was clawin' his back."

"Vigilantes, eh?"

"*Aw,* no. Didn't you hear he had had the sign of the hawk put on him?"

"What's the sign, anyway?"

"Why, I've seen one of 'em. A mighty neat made little bird that's like a hawk. Handsome Harry sticks it on any gent he's downed."

"What for, I'd like to know?"

"Well," said the first speaker, "I figger it's like this. Delancey seems to fight fair. He's never gone after a gent that didn't have a chance to fill his hand. An' when he drops a man, he puts a signature on him, as you might say."

"He didn't sign the Morgantown murders," remarked the other.

"Because he didn't do 'em! You can lay to that. The kid is straight, I tell you. Poison, sure. But straight, if you foller my drift."

Ching Wo went softly on through the night for a stroll in the woods. He was satisfied with this little conversation, for it justified the character that he had tried to maintain under his false name. He was no mere murderer, to these men; they recognized his qualities and gave him credit for them.

He smiled when he thought of Doc Peters, rushing

away from San Salvadore, and only returning when he had managed to gather together a bodyguard of friends, no doubt.

But there was a somber meaning in this, also. For if men took him so seriously, they would begin to make life much harder. His face, his voice, his ways of action were becoming known to greater numbers.

At length Ching felt it was time to return to his work, and, in fact, when he went back to the hotel, he found every light had been extinguished.

He waited for a moment before the hotel. Gradually he could hear the snores of many heavy slumberers. This was reassuring, so he hesitated no longer, but went to the verandah and climbed cat-like up the first pillar. It was made of a pole with the bark left on, giving him an excellent handhold and leg grip. Soon he was on the verandah roof.

Here he had to go with a redoubled caution, for he knew that the shakes with which it was covered were dry with the summer heat, and would *crackle* more than twigs breaking underfoot, unless he went as softly as a snake.

Long minutes went by, as Ching edged his way up the slope of the verandah roof, but not a sound did he allow to come from beneath him, in spite of the pressure of his weight.

He was just beneath the corner window when a voice called out loudly from a nearby room: "Shanks! Shanks! I give up!"

There was a growling answer: "What the hell?"

"I had a dream," said an apologetic answering voice.

"You have another dream like that and I'll bust you one, you poor thickhead!"

Cots *creaked* as the disturbed sleepers turned. Beneath the corner window the boy lay, still as a watching cat, waiting, waiting through the long minutes, until he heard the beginning of a new snore. Then he rose to his knees.

The window was not open sufficiently for him to pass through. He examined the frame of it with what care he could, having to feel with his fingers, since the light was too dim for seeing. He could tell that the frame was warped. For that very reason, no doubt, the window had not been thrust up higher.

And now the youth began a more difficult labor. He had to lift hard, but, as he lifted, he had to make sure that the sash did not give with a sudden *screech* under the weight of his hand. It was a simple thing, and yet of the utmost delicacy.

Moreover, the strength of his exertions must not make him pant, for sailors, as he knew, may be light sleepers.

Twice and again Ching had to pause, breathing with care of the pine-scented air, and listening, listening. Again he resumed the work, and finally the window began to give, creeping little by little up until it was wide enough for him to enter.

Again he paused, waited for his breathing to grow quiet. Then, putting his head through the gap, he threw his very soul before him into the darkness of the room.

It was very black. He could only make out the shape of a bed in the center of the eastern wall. It was a very small chamber, and for that reason there was only the one cot. For this, also, he was thankful. He felt sure that the man he sought was delivered utterly into his hands.

Then he slipped a leg through, found the floor, and stepped softly in.

One step, now, would bring him to his prey. The heart of Ching Wo was as hard as a flint.

From the corner beside the window he heard a faint *click*, and a torrent of light blazed at him from the suddenly unhooded lantern.

It dazed Ching Wo, but, even when dazed, his instinct told him what to do. He dropped for the floor as though the shaft of light had been a sword passing through his heart, and, as he dropped, the roar of a gun filled the room!

XXI

Ching Wo had not fallen prone, but on hands and knees, and from them he leaped up under the flare of the lantern light as the gun barked again. The bullet nicked his ear like the sting of a wasp, and then Ching was grappling with his enemy.

This big man's frame was even more huge than Ching had expected. His chest was as big and as hard as the girth of a heavy barrel. The muscles of his arms were like quivering rubber.

"You sneakin' greaser!" gasped the man in the dark. "I'm gonna have the stranglin' of you!"

One hand was at Ching's throat.

The two shots had filled the whole house with an uproar. From the next room came a thundering tumult, and curses boomed as loudly as though the thin partition were not between the two chambers.

But that iron hand on the boy's throat was the first danger, and Ching knew exactly how to meet it. There are ways of paralyzing muscles that every expert in the art of *jujitsu* knows, and the youth was proficient. With the edge of his stiffened hand, as with a cleaver, he struck heavily across the rigid muscles of the man's upper arm. The nerves were paralyzed by the shock, and the fingers on Ching's throat turned to nerveless lumps.

With an oath and a grunt the big man thrust the boy away and sent him reeling, then followed in headlong charge.

"For Wei Sung," said Ching, snarling his mother's name. "You die for Wei Sung!"

"Open up!" thundered a voice, rattling the doorknob.

The big fellow, as he reached Ching, smote with all the force of his remaining useful arm, but it was for this Ching was waiting. A thousand times he had practiced the trick with his professor. The heart of *jujitsu* is to make the enemy's strength defeat him, and he used that system now.

For as the arm shot at him, he swayed his head to one side and whirled his body like a top. That big arm he grappled and swayed his shoulder against it.

The result was only what he had seen happen twenty times in the lessons. 200 trained and hardened pounds of muscle, made helpless by their own forward rush, were heaved over Ching's shoulder. The monster *crashed* with a splintering force upon the floor, groaned, and lay still.

And that moment, under the impact of lurching shoulders, the door was burst open. A light gleamed and showed Ching Wo leaning over the prostrate man with knife poised for the death stroke.

Even then he had time and would have driven the blow home. What did his own life matter if this work were accomplished? But the lantern glow showed him not the face of Captain Foster, but a smooth-shaven young Hercules, his eyes closed, his mouth open from the shock of his fall.

Ching turned and ran for the open window. A bullet split the pane above when he dived through. As he rolled down the verandah roof another bullet *cracked* through the shakes beside his head. But then he tumbled over the edge, hung half an instant by his hands, and dropped to the ground as silently as possible.

Two half-dressed men instantly collared him. "Who the hell are you?" they roared.

"Murder!" gasped Ching, becoming limp in their grasp. "They're murdering somebody. . . ."

"Come on, Charlie," grunted one of his captors. "This here is only a paralyzed damn' tenderfoot."

They charged back indoors.

Ching Wo passed unhindered around the side of the house and raced for the woods, with the moon's dim light gleaming through topmost branches of the trees.

He heard a shout behind him.

"There he goes! There, d'you see? For the trees! Our hosses an' foller the sneak . . . !"

"Hosses! Hosses!"

Every man at Slater's Hotel had rushed out into the dark, and now the current swept toward the stables.

Ching Wo ran fast.

There would be draft animals, sluggish mules, and short-striding Indian ponies in those stables, he knew, but there were also sure to be some blood horses that might make even El Rey work hard.

He gained the place where he had left the stallion. El Rey pitched to his feet as his master came. On the back of the noble steed he threw the saddle and tugged the cinches taut. As Ching leaped into the stirrups, he heard the *crash* of many horses and riders striking the outer brush of the wood and coming straight on at him in one headlong volley.

Ching had erred, as he well realized now.

He should have run from the house in a false direction, and then, most easily, he could have eluded them in the woods and gained El Rey.

But now they had their horses beneath them, open woods through which to hunt, and the light of the moon to show them the way. Under his tight lips, Ching's teeth flashed as he gave El Rey his head, and off they darted.

He headed up the right-hand slough. The going would be slower if he kept to the trees, but he hoped they might not find him.

The youth was wrong. He had not ridden a quarter of a mile before he could hear them shouting behind him. Thereupon he broke out into the open and headed south—any direction, so long as it was away from the road to Buffalo Flat.

They followed into the open with a yell—a dozen men on straining horses, and the long, unfenced flat before them. It must be a clear race, therefore, in which honest blood and long legs would tell.

So the fugitive steadied El Rey, gave him a little pull to balance him in his striding, and then looked back.

Of the dozen, five were left. The rest were falling rapidly to the rear, but these five must be riding Kentucky blood, at least. By the rhythm of their galloping, Ching could tell the magnificent striding of those good horses, and instinctively he touched his rifle butt.

But it seemed as much a murder to shoot down such animals as these as it would have been to turn his gun upon white man or yellow. Ching settled himself to the work of riding and let El Rey take another mile at burning speed.

Two more had fallen back, then. They were not so far behind as to be out of the race, but they were losing. The fugitive sighed, however, as he noted that the leaders apparently had not lost a yard. Neither did one quirt flash in the moonlight. They were hand-riding their mounts, which meant that all of them were fresh.

El Rey already had done ten miles this day, no matter how leisurely.

And yet with pricking ears he ran, the fields flowing like water beneath his hoofs as he pressed on the bit and asked for more rein, but more rein he should not have. For a short sprint would kill off the king of horses, and well Ching Wo realized it.

They came to a crossing of many fences, where someone had closed in farm land in a rich bottom, and Ching sent his gray straight at the barriers, for he knew how the stallion could jump. Over they soared, and over and over, ever in stride.

As they left the ranch house, dark and squat upon their right, Ching looked back and saw two horsemen following him. The others were blotted out behind. At that he laughed fiercely. These two had ridden well and boldly, but did they think they were dealing with some skulking fox?

Low foothills were rising ahead, and, as Ching Wo entered them, he aimed for a copse of oaks that topped the nearest hill. Into that he rode, turned El Rey about, and sent a bullet whistling over the heads of the pursuers.

They split apart like water on a rock, one to one side and one to the other.

Ching fired again, and knew his bullet had kicked up rocks under the feet of the left-hand man.

They fell back, milled around for a moment, and then stood still. They would wait to be reinforced by the other riders, who now were darkly streaking across the distant fields.

Ching smiled, for he knew the end had come. Taking El Rey out of the woods, he jogged him gently into a hollow at right angles to his original line of flight. Softly he went on to another grove of trees, and there halted.

The youth was not ten minutes in the place before he saw the five riders sweep out of the grove he had just left. Once more they halted, then drew together as in consultation, but at length they turned gloomily back. They took the hollow, as being easier ground.

Ching grew tense. Yet he did not leave his cover. They had not the attitude now of hunters keen upon a scent, but of beaten men.

They came so close that he could study the horses, although the men's faces were lost in the shadows of their broad-brimmed hats. Ching had been right. Two of the horses, at least, were clean-limbed thorough-breds, and of them he could hear their riders speak, less than fifty feet from the trees.

"That gray is a flyer," said one. "I gave everything the Jester had to those fences, but I didn't gain an inch."

"I never thought," replied another, "that we'd meet that kind of blood in this locality. We might have left our hosses home, Bud, and bought others out here."

There was some consolation for them, however, for a third member of the party spoke up at once.

"You boys take this easy. I knew when we started that we'd never catch him. But I wanted to see what this half-breed of mine would do, and I'm satisfied."

"You knew we'd never catch him?"

"Why, man, that's the gray hoss of Handsome Harry! That's what it is, or I'm a liar. They ain't two hosses in California of that color and speed."

"Handsome Harry! He ain't one of these midnight murderers, I've been told."

"You been told? Well, tonight we've seen somethin' else, ain't we?"

They passed on out of earshot, and Ching Wo, compressing his lips, knew that the escutcheon of Harry Delancey had been blackened, indeed, by this unlucky night's work. He would have to work hard to make it seem clean again.

XXII

Meanwhile, at Slater's Hotel, affairs were taking place that were of importance to Ching Wo, although he knew it not. For his own part, he was drifting easily across the countryside, toward Buffalo Flat, with a great unease in his mind. It was necessary for him to tell his father two things.

The first was that he had made the attempt to kill the enemy, but had failed because the wrong man was in the room he entered, and because that man was armed and prepared for danger. The second thing to note was that Handsome Harry Delancey was, for the first time, apt to be charged with an underhanded murderous attack.

Obviously it was to the advantage of both Ching and

Li Wo to keep the repute of Handsome Harry as free from stain as possible, as long as it was necessary for the boy to seek refuge repeatedly in the disguise that that assumed personality gave to him.

So Ching cantered on the gray stallion through the moonlight, and across the stripes of oak- and willow-grown sloughs that barred the country with darkness, toward the distant river, while, in Slater's Hotel, Captain Foster was holding an inquiry.

It was Tim Dodd who had been attacked in the room where the skipper had at first intended to sleep, and from which he had gone at the last minute.

But it was difficult for Foster to interview Tim at this moment, since the poor man lay groaning, with a broken head. However, Sandy Webb, the boson, taking care of the injured seaman, had heard all that Tim had to say up to the present moment.

Captain Foster sent for Sandy, and they conversed in low voices on the verandah of the hotel.

Said the captain: "Boson, this is a thing I wouldn't have believed. Here's one of the best men I found in harbor . . . a man worthy to be signed as a third mate . . . a fellow who's said to have beaten a whole ship's crew into order with his fists . . . that's what they said of Tim Dodd. And now look what's happened to him . . . from a youth half his size!"

Captain Foster seemed nonplussed for a moment. "If Tim Dodd dies from this. . . ."

"He won't die, sir," Sandy replied. "The bones of his head are a mite sprung, that's all."

"He was warned, he was warned," said the captain with heat. "I told the fool what he might expect. Did I bring the five of you upcountry with me for the sake of a lark? No, no, boson, I brought you because I think I'm in as much danger as ever was a ship that tried to sail Strait Le Maire in a blind fog. From the moment when I saw that the Chinamen were trailing me and skulking behind me in San Francisco streets, I knew what I was in for. What was tried on Tim Dodd was intended for me . . . and all that saved the man was the sight of his face . . . which was not mine."

Foster strode back and forth a moment, collecting his thoughts. "And now Tim is in a bad way?"

"Aye, sir," said Sandy Webb. "But there's somethin' mysterious, as they say, about this here go. It ain't a broken head that makes Tim groan, but it's the broken heart inside of him."

"Why is his heart broken, then?" the captain inquired patiently, although he was not a patient man.

"It was like this, Tim says. He set himself down in the corner. He had a hooded dark lantern at his feet an' a good Colt's revolver in his hand. . . ."

"Can he shoot?"

"He can, sir. I seen him only yesterday split an apple at fifteen paces. Well, sir, while he set there, he thought somethin' come to the window. He couldn't be sure for a while, but pretty soon he made out that the window was raisin', without no sound. An' that made his flesh crawl pretty bad, because he'd tried to raise that window himself the night before, an' it had stuck.

Well, sir, anyway, Tim seen the sash creepin' up, slow an' gradual, an' it was a mighty shock to him. Then he thinks that he'll go an' see what's there, but then he says to himself that he won't, but he'll just sit tight an' wait an' catch the thing if it tries to come into the room, because Tim knew he'd been put there in case somebody was to try on him what was meant for you, sir."

"Go on, boson, and be brief."

"I'll be brief, then. The window opened, an' in slides a man without no sound, like a feather blowin', or a ghost."

"Rot!" cried the captain. "What are you trying to tell me?"

"Rot, sir, you may well say, an' so said Tim a minute later. But first he opened his lamp, an' by the light of it he whanged away at this stranger that was a youngster, sort of slender, lookin' fast, but not very solid. He had long black hair. Twice Tim fired. At the first shot the gent fell, but he jumped off of the floor like a wildcat an' come in at Tim.

"'If that's your game,' says Tim to himself, 'I'll tear out your windpipe,' an' he took the feller by the throat. But all at once he was hit across the upper arm an' his hand turned numb. With the other hand he pushed the feller away an' rushed at him, an', while he was rushin', he heard this here stranger say, mighty clear an' distinct . . . 'For Wei Sung. You die for Wei Sung.'

"Then Tim hit at him, but all at once he found himself bein' heaved into the air, an' he landed with a

158

whack that knocked the wits out of him, clean an' entire. Now, sir, that's Tim's story, an' he swears by it, an' he ain't a lyin' man."

"Wei Sung," repeated the captain slowly. "Wei Sung. I don't think I've ever heard of the name before. Wei Sung?"

He shook his head.

"All chinks look alike," declared the boson, "an' the chink names sound all the same to us. But they don't forget the way we do."

Several men came in from the stable, cursing and talking to one another.

"They're the boys that did the riding," said the captain. "I almost knew they'd have no luck. Well, my friends, who was it?"

The reply came promptly: "Handsome Harry Delancey."

"And you caught him?"

"He was ridin' the wind in the shape of his gray hoss. We didn't catch him."

They filed into the house, heedless of the noise they made, as men are who have tried hard and failed.

The captain muttered aloud, so that the boson could hear him: "Wei Sung . . . Chinese money . . . and a white gunman hired."

XXIII

In Canary Cañon, Stephen Linton had put up his lean-to against the side of the cliff. It consisted of a few poles made out of freshly cut saplings, with canvas stretched over them. A mere tent—a rude tent, at that.

Linton himself was now drawing up the girths of a pack mule, loaded down with samples of what he hoped would prove rich ore, to take to the assay office in San Salvadore. The tent's front flaps were thrown wide, and Margery Linton could be seen within, rolling out biscuit dough and keeping an eye upon the ramshackle stove that had been improvised in a corner of the shelter.

"Come give me a hand!" called Linton, sweating and shaking his head. "There's no strength in my shoulders this morning, Margery."

"I'll give you a hand," answered a voice from among the rocks, and Linton saw Handsome Harry Delancey come riding up among the rocks on a splendid red roan stallion.

It was not the first time Ching had visited the miner. Margery ran to the entrance and waved a flour-whitened hand.

Ching, hat in hand, bowed until his long black curls touched the saddle bow. Then he dismounted and drew up the cinches of the pack animal with one pull, while Linton looked on with grudging admiration.

"Where do you get the strength in those lean shoulders of yours?" he asked, laying a hand on the boy's arm familiarly.

Under his touch Linton felt the working of the long strings of muscles, hard as rubber, and he exclaimed with surprise: "If you're as lazy a fellow as you pretend, Delancey, how do you keep so fit?"

"By pulling on cinches," Ching answered with a smile. "How are they working?"

He pointed to a pair of Mexicans who, a little distance down the slope, were busily sinking a drill into soft rock. The clangor of the hammer on the drill head raised musical echoes that rolled softly from wall to wall of the valley in the thin mountain air.

"Like that," said Linton. "They work like that all day long."

"But we're half afraid of them," Margery declared. "They have a pretty black look, you know."

"They look like murder," said Linton frankly. "I'd suspect them of anything if you hadn't sent them to me."

"They've done murder," Ching replied.

"Murder?" gasped the girl.

"That's why they're working for you, instead of trying to stake out their own claims. They don't want to call attention to themselves."

"You don't mean murder!" exclaimed Linton. "You don't mean you've sent me a pair of murderers?"

"They won't harm you," Ching Wo replied. "They know I sent them here in the first place."

"Does that guarantee them?"

"In a way. You see, they've been hunted before, and they don't want to be hunted again."

Linton looked at the girl, who, in turn, stared curiously at Ching. She and her father had often talked with him, but they could not understand him. They could not help looking down at the busy Mexicans and wondering.

"If you've nothing better to do," Linton told the boy, "stay here till I come back from town. I'd rather not leave Margery alone in the valley with that pair."

"She's not alone," said Ching, pointing to busy prospectors above and below the claim, some distance away. "But I'll remain here."

He and the girl watched Linton walk off down the valley, leading the mule. Then they turned back into the tent, regardless of a figure that slipped closer among the rocks, until it was crouched close to the rear wall of the tent, in easy earshot. This was Li Wo, minus his silks, dressed roughly as any laborer in the mines. Patiently he sat there; patiently he listened.

Ching Wo, inside the tent, sat down on a stool and watched the girl working the dough.

"You have a new horse," she said. "It looks almost as fine as El Rey."

"It is as fine," Ching responded, "because it's the same horse."

Margery looked up at him, startled, and then smiled. "How did you manage that?"

"Why, the same way you'd guess. It's a good, fast

dye. People were beginning to recognize the gray too easily."

At this she fell silent and began to cut out the biscuits with the top of a baking powder tin, dipping the tin into flour each time, so that it would not stick to the dough.

"It was by the gray horse that they tied you to that affair at Slater's Crossing, wasn't it?" the girl asked presently, without looking up.

"Ah, yes," Ching responded in an unconcerned voice. "It was by the horse that they knew me."

"That they knew you!" she exclaimed. "Are you admitting . . . ?"

"Oh, that I was there? Of course.

She looked up, utterly aghast. "But they said . . . you went into Captain Foster's room . . . at night . . . to . . . to murder him, Harry."

"Not a bit," was the reply. "I went in to give him a fair chance for his life."

She merely stared, trying in vain to understand that viewpoint. Then she made a wry face. "He told Dad you were hired by Chinamen."

At this the boy leaned a little forward and smiled at her. "You don't like Chinamen, Margery?"

"I? Like them? No, I. . . ."

Ching looked down thoughtfully. "I have several Chinese friends."

"Not really friends," she said.

"Why not?" he parried.

"Chinamen?" she echoed incredulously.

"You think of the laborers . . . common, stupid fellows. But there are Chinamen who I have felt were a good deal above me."

Ching saw the girl shake her head and look past him through the open flaps of the tent, and across the ravine to the pines that darkened the opposite bluff. In this small silence they were able to hear the talking of the stream in the bottom of the valley, and again the clangor of the hammer on the drill head, sounding wonderfully far away.

So Margery looked off, but did not seem to find what she was looking for.

"Once," she said, "I heard of a white girl . . . of good family, too . . . who married one of the creatures. Think of that!"

"Well . . . I can think of it," Ching replied. "Who did she marry?"

"Oh, some Mandarin or other. I don't know. With long fingernails, I suppose."

"A bad-hearted man, Margery?" he asked icily.

"I don't know. It hardly matters. I simply don't like to have them around, you know."

Ching was silent. It was exquisite torture, but he prolonged it. "I've known a Chinaman who I respect as much as I do my own father," he said.

"Have you, Harry? But you're a romanticist, of course."

She said it half smiling, half sneering.

The young man watched her face, answering gravely: "Well, I won't try to convince you today."

"Don't ever try," she insisted. "Besides, there's a lot else to talk about."

"Ah?" he said half dreamily. There was a pause, how long he did not know.

Suddenly her voice broke in on him. "Do you know something, Harry?"

"Ah?" he said again.

"When you sit there with your head tipped back and that unhuman smile on your lips, you look exactly like a Buddha."

He started. "I?"

"Yes. I mean it. Most of the time you're just like any other boy . . . but now and again it's like a peek into an Oriental temple. It scares me. Makes me think of human sacrifice and that sort of thing."

"I'm sorry," Ching replied.

"You're not very jolly today," she remarked.

"Ah," said Ching, "perhaps I'm not."

He mused again with the faint, half smile that bewildered and abashed Margery.

"You're troubled about something," she insisted.

"Yes," he admitted.

She waited, watching him so earnestly that she forgot the pan of biscuits, now ready for the fire.

"In fact," said Ching Wo, "I would like to talk to you because of my trouble."

"I would do what I could," Margery reassured him, with all the good will in the world—such good will that her voice trembled a little.

"Then I'll tell you," he said. "I've fallen in love."

Ching did not seem to be looking at Margery, but rather at the ground and at his own thought, but he saw she had grown rigid and the color had sunk down in her face. He carefully avoided the frightened, staring eyes that were fixed upon him, and the colorless parted lips.

"I have fallen in love with a beautiful young Chinese girl," said Ching Wo, waiting for the lie to take effect.

Margery Linton turned away suddenly, wresting herself around, as it were. Opening the door of the oven, she thrust in the pan of biscuits and slammed the door with a great *crash*.

"A Chinese girl?" she repeated, with her back still turned to him.

He reflected on the greatness of his lie, while he stared at her hungrily. His eyes embraced her body and her very soul, drawing them close to his heart.

"After what you said about the Chinese," Ching explained, "I thought I'd better tell you the truth."

"Do you want to open my eyes about those people?" she inquired.

"I'm afraid I couldn't do that," he said. "But at a time like this, a man needs to have a woman to advise him, don't you think?"

"I suppose he does." Her voice was almost inaudible.

"And I, lacking a mother, wondered where I could go. So I decided I'd come to you, Margery. If you won't mind listening. . . ."

"Oh, no," she said. "Of course I will listen gladly, if

you find . . . I don't know how I could be of the slightest help, though. But . . . is she beautiful, really, Harry?"

"She is more beautiful to me than all the other beauty in the world."

"Ah . . . well. . . ." Margery sighed. "But how can I help you?"

"Why, the trouble is, she pays no attention to me."

"Doesn't she?"

"No, not a bit. To her I'm simply a freak . . . a queer fellow . . . interesting, but not important. She laughs at me a good deal."

"I didn't know," the girl murmured thoughtfully, "that Chinese maidens were allowed to see men?"

"She has been raised in this country, which makes a great difference. She's given freedom like a Western woman."

"I'm glad to hear that," said Margery. Then she broke out: "But if you married her . . . and if you had children . . . how do you think Americans would feel about . . . about half-breeds? I beg your pardon, Harry. I hope that isn't a rude thing to say."

"For my part, I don't care what the Americans may think. But what difference does it make?"

"Oh," she cried, "to be neither one thing nor another . . . but something between two races! To have a girl with a yellow skin and a boy with a white one! I . . . I don't want to think of it!" she concluded with horror.

"She's a charming girl to look at," Ching persisted.

He said it with a sudden change of voice, so that the

girl started. Looking at him, she saw his eyes were on fire, and she flushed warmly.

"You *are* in love!"

"If I could win her heart," Ching responded, "I wouldn't care a whit about the consequences in the minds of other people. I would make her happy."

"And why won't she listen to you, Harry?"

"Well, for one thing, she doesn't think I lead a very safe sort of a life . . . this galloping about the face of the landscape, she thinks rather a bad way of making a living."

"Do you wonder at that? I'm glad she has a practical mind," said Margery, something like spite in her voice.

"She doesn't approve of my way of living at all," Ching continued. "She forgets I could change that, afterwards."

"And what would you do, then?"

"Anything that other men can do. For her sake I'd attempt anything. In China or in New York, I don't care which. I would find a way of managing things."

"I think you would," Margery agreed.

"But my work is to win her . . . to break down the wall . . . to make her on fire with love, if I can."

"Does her father allow you to see her when you choose?"

"Oh, yes. We even go riding together."

"Really? She doesn't have bound feet, then, and that sort of thing?"

"Oh, no. She's like . . . why, she's as free and easy as you are, Margery. And her feet haven't been deformed.

Her parents have lived in California for a long time, you see. She speaks English better than she does Chinese."

"Does she, really? But how can I help you, Harry?"

"I've never tried to talk seriously to a girl before . . . and I've been trying to compose a letter to her. Would you listen to it?"

She started. "I'm no critic. I don't know much about such things. But I'll try my best." She braced herself with a slight frown of attention.

Ching, with his head tilted back a little, and his eyes half closed, began to speak in a soft, rhythmical voice: "Most beautiful and most dear . . . in all the days since I have met you, eye to eye, and voice to voice, you have given me much sadness."

He paused.

"I don't know," Margery commented in a barely audible voice. "It has a pleasant sound, but should you begin by speaking about sadness?"

"Well, that's what I'd like to have you do . . . criticize every part for me, you know."

"I'll try," she said. "Go on."

Ching continued: "Every step in your father's house is a moment of sweet pain to me, and, when the cups of tea are uncovered, then I breathe sorrow and delight at one moment. When I hear the soft patter of padded shoes upon the floor, and the whisper of the fountain in your garden, and, when I smell the honeysuckle that grows against the northern wall, where the bees are always at work in the sun . . . these things to me are you. I find in them the sound of your own step, of your own whispering garment, and the murmur of your voice in the distance. But in those happier days, my dear, when I went out from your father's house, I could forget you a little. When the door had closed, the same wind that blew the white clouds over the sky blew the thoughts even of you beneath the horizon. But all of this has changed since you rode with me through the pine trees by night. . . ."

"Through the pine trees!" Margery gasped.

"Ah, yes, because, you see, she and I rode together the other evening through the woods together."

"Alone?"

Her father was with us, but he lagged a good deal behind. He's not a very good horseman."

"Go on," said Margery faintly.

"Since you rode with me through the pine trees by night, I never can leave you, for I find the sweetness of your hair in the breath from the pines, and sometimes I stop my horse on the road, because the sound of the water falling in the next valley makes me think of your laughter.

"Dearest and most beautiful, show me some kindness. I am so sad that I do not care for the truth which you would show to braver men . . . but even if you do despite me, try to be gentle.

"If I am not of your people, still I have a heart which loves you, and because of that, you should remember that into the least small pool the heavens will pour down a little of their blue." He paused again. "I cannot think of a proper way of ending it."

The girl did not answer.

"But perhaps you'll suggest one, Margery."

She replied in a broken voice: "I've started crying. I don't know why. But it makes me broken-hearted to think of you thrown away on . . . a Chinese maiden. Harry, Harry, if only you will wait, you may find it's a silly fancy. It's your first love, and perhaps not your last one."

"Ah?" Ching responded simply. "Do you believe people change, as you say?"

"Why," replied Margery, "I'd almost wager that you will."

"And the letter?"

"It's too beautiful for her. She'd never understand."

"Don't you think so?" he asked in the voice of one being instructed.

"I know she wouldn't. I . . . I wouldn't send it at all."

"You understand a great deal more about such things than I do," said Ching. "I think I should let you tell me what to do."

XXIV

Li Wo had waited patiently through all of this part of the conversation, although his eyes had begun to burn like the eyes of a hunting cat.

But now he rose, almost frightened by the possibility that the boy might come out and find him there. The wily father could penetrate the simple riddle of Ching Wo, who was talking of no other woman, but indi-

171

rectly and subtly making love to beautiful Margery Linton herself.

Now, having heard enough to fix this thing in his mind, Li Wo slipped away among the rocks that littered the whole valley and that had made it such a difficult task for Linton to rediscover the lead from which he had taken the valuable ore before.

An earthquake had unsettled the whole southern wall of the ravine and thrown down tens of thousands of tons of great boulders that rolled as far as the creek itself. This day Linton thought he had found what he wanted, and for that reason he had gone in with the mule load of ore to the assay office.

Li Wo, who had heard of the story, looked enviously here and there among the great rocks, as he went slowly back toward San Salvadore. All that the white men did was to him a torment. Every pound of gold they drained from the earth was a curse to him, for his hatred of the race burned like a poison through his veins.

But this day Li Wo had learned the worst of all.

He knew Ching's passion and the headlong nature, barely held in check by that worship of his father as a semi-divine being that the Chinese manners teach, and which Li Wo particularly had insisted upon from the very first.

But now the youth had fallen deeply in love with a white woman, and Li Wo feared Ching would slip through his hands like sand through careless fingers. He groaned and gnashed his teeth.

He had seen, from the first, that in Ching he had a priceless tool, which he had labored many years to perfect and make into a sharp-edged instrument.

He had beggared himself in securing the best masters to teach the lad's mind and to instruct his body in every deadly and graceful science of weapons and of the *jujitsu*.

The discovery of John Glendon, a cultured hermit in the woods, had been priceless, in that it had enabled Li Wo to form the other half of Ching's nature into the semblance of a Westerner. That done, the youth could step out into the world in a double rôle and slip from one to the other with a perfect ease.

Li Wo and his future ease were both committed to the hands of Ching, and of late he could not have wished for more than the boy brought in to him. Thousands of dollars had flowed as a ceaseless current, and like a well-trained cormorant, all that the lad caught was virtuously brought home to his father.

But now all the brightness and the luxurious idleness of his future were endangered by the face of a pretty girl of the white race. Ten thousand devils filled the soul of Li Wo, who wondered where he should turn first.

He came into sight of San Salvadore, in the valley beneath the ravine's mouth, and there he paused to curse the white man and all his works.

Li Wo was worked into such a grand fury that his mind was still clouded by the fumes of it as he descended into the town. In fact, he barely managed to dodge from under the hoofs of a galloping horse at the entrance to San Salvadore's main street.

The rider's loud, insulting laughter increased the red cloud that swirled across the brain of Li Wo. He wished fiercely that Ching were with him at that moment. Oh, well for the noisy rider that Ching had not seen and heard.

The angry old man went on down the street aimlessly, filled with his thoughts, his lips twitching with words and his eyes fixed straight ahead, when a great voice shattered his evil dream. A mighty hand gripped him by the arms, and he looked up into the face of big Captain Malcolm Foster, square-trimmed beard and all.

Distinctly out of the past he could remember that face. Except for the wrinkles about the eyes, it was the same. Worse than that, Captain Foster seemed to remember him still, despite the lapse of years.

"It's the chink devil . . . the chink murderer!" boomed the captain. "Here, boson, put a splice on his hands and tie them together. We'll have him into the jail in short order. I hear that the sheriff's in town today."

Li Wo, turned into a statue, stood fast and said not a word. Around him gathered a pool of the curious—rough-handed miners, sleek-faced gamblers, all the crowd of idlers that drifted every day through San Salvadore.

"That's Foster," he heard someone say. "That's Captain Foster, who Delancey went after a while ago."

The skipper heard the voice and answered at once.

"I'm Malcolm Foster, and I've caught the Chinese rat who hired Delancey to cut my throat. I'll have the sheriff take care of him."

"He hired Delancey? Delancey's not the sort to be hired by a chink," was the answer.

"I tell you, I have the proof," said Foster aggressively. "Delancey mentioned a name when he thought it was I he had to deal with. There's no doubt about it. This is the man."

The boson already, with a bit of the cord that is never absent from a sailor's pockets, had lashed the Chinaman's wrists together behind his back.

Then Li Wo spoke in perfect English: "My friends, there is some great mistake. I never have seen this gentleman before, and I'm sure he never has seen me."

"You lie!" bellowed the captain, infuriated. "I remember on the ship that you could speak good English even then. It's the man, or I'm a fool. I tell you, your name is Li Wo, and you. . . ."

"Li Wo!" said one of the men in the gathering crowd. "It's Li Wo, right enough. I've seen him twenty times. He's one of the rich chinks from Buffalo Flat."

Foster's recognition of the captive's name had an immediate effect.

One lank, lofty, sour-faced man pushed into the central circle.

"I dunno," he began, "but what this here is a good time for us to ask a few questions, Cap'n Foster, which I guess is your name."

"It is," the captain admitted rather suspiciously.

"Well, the idea is kind of like this," explained the tall man. "We got a jail in this here town, an' we got a right bang-up sheriff. But they's a sort of a vacancy in the line of judges."

"Vacancy?" queried the captain.

"The air don't seem to be no good for a real judge," said the stranger sadly. "We lost one day before yesterday, an' we lost another last week. The way things have carried on here, it don't seem likely we're gonna have another with us for quite a spell."

Foster smiled. "You mean the legal judges have been killed? Is that it?"

"It's the dog-gone' unfortunate truth," said the other, with the same set jaw and determined manner. "Now, if you was to take over that chink, there, to the jail, there wouldn't be nothin' to do with him except to lock him up, which would cause a mighty lot of trouble to Sheriff Lefty Wilson, to set around an' entertain him. An' the sheriff, I gotta say, has other things needin' his attention in this town, outside of chinks."

"I understand." Foster nodded. Then he turned to Li Wo, who stood with a face frozen by fear. "If you mean that he ought to be turned over to vigilantes. . . ."

"That's what I mean," said the tall man.

"I don't want to be a party to any mob murders," Foster objected. "Is there an organized vigilante body here?"

"There is," said the tall man.

"And who's the head of it?"

"Which the head an' the chairman of it all is me,

an' I might interduce myself. I'm Jim Bone."

The captain shook hands with him.

"I dunno," said Jim Bone, "that you'd wanna go ahead with this here job, Cap'n Foster, unless you had what satisfied you as bang-up, honest-to-God truth on your side of it?"

Li Wo cried suddenly, his voice choked and thin with fear: "He has no proof! He has no proof! Gentlemen, gentlemen, will you listen to a poor Chinaman when he tries to tell you the truth, and if. . . ."

The heavy, lank hand of Jim Bone struck Li Wo heavily across the mouth and silenced him.

"I dunno," said Bone, "but I reckon that the time ain't come quite yet when a chink can crow right up like a rooster in the middle of the street here in San Salvadore. You shut yer face," he added to Li Wo, his drawl never varying, no matter how violent might be the sentiments he uttered. "You're gonna have your chance, but not till you're standin' under the judgment tree. Cap'n Foster, if you got your proofs in mind, we'll go ahead to that there tree right now, and we'll have a trial of this here yaller rat. If he ain't guilty, he ought to be. An', anyways, there's a lot more yaller chinks in this state than is wanted."

With this unprejudiced speech the judge waved to the crowd. The savage blood of San Salvadore was instantly burning, and with a chorus of wild shouts a guard of death assembled. Li Wo walked in the middle of a ravening tumult, with blood streaking slowly down his face from the wounded lip.

XXV

The judgment tree was a big oak, which spread its branches to either side on the bank of San Salvadore Creek, just below the town. It was a magnificent tree, with such a huge ceiling of limbs and of leaves that even when a rain sprang up, the court and the audience still could remain in session.

All about it were scattered rocks of sizes convenient to be used as chairs. Jim Bone took an armchair of natural rock in the center of the scene and immediately began presiding.

He said: "Masters, have you had a drink this morning?"

"No," replied a red-shirted miner.

"Then you're the clerk," instructed Jim Bone. "You try to recollect the important things that may be said, if they's anything really important that can be said about a yaller chink. Didn't I see Two-Gun Hendricks over yonder? Hey, Hendricks!"

A little nervous man came forward, glancing to right and left, asking pardon of everyone whose elbow he touched. But when he was on the edge of the circle, he fixed upon Bone the steadiest pair of gray eyes in the world.

"You called me?" he asked.

"Hendricks, you're the sergeant-at-arms. You know what that means?"

"No, I don't."

"It means you keep order. If anybody starts a ruction, you stop it."

Hendricks passed the tip of his tongue over his pale lips. "I'll do what I can."

And at once he faded back into the crowd, but everyone knew he was there. Every man, after a moment, was convinced that the deadly little fighter was just behind his back. Never was there a more orderly mob in San Salvadore than upon this day.

Now we want a jury," said Jim Bone. "The chink can pick one man, and you pick another, Cap'n Foster. You start in."

Captain Foster was grim and stern, a man fond of his own way, but it was his first acquaintance with lynch rule. So he stood forth and made a little speech.

"Gentlemen, I don't know what legal jurisdiction, if any, is vested in a court of this nature. . . ."

"Don't you start worryin' about that," interrupted Jim Bone. "Them that we hang are as dead as though the Supreme Court had hung 'em up, an' don't you doubt it. They may kick a little longer, but they all need plantin' afterward."

"I don't doubt that," said the captain. "This seems to be the custom of the land, and I accept it. I'm convinced that Li Wo is a scoundrel and hired a man to murder me, but, at the same time, I don't want to take advantage of any prejudice against his people in order to obtain a conviction. I would like to select unprejudiced men to hear the evidence in this case, but, since I don't know my fellow citizens of San Salvadore, I think I should leave the choosing to an experienced man like the judge. Mister Bone, will you act for me in naming my half of the jury?"

Said Jim Bone: "This here is a dog-gone' fair an' open act. It's plain to see that Cap'n Foster is a gentleman, an' is sure gonna be given his rights in this here town."

There was a murmur of agreement.

"What's fair for a white man is fair for a Chinaman," continued "Judge" Bone. "So I'll name the whole jury."

This he did, straightway selecting twelve men with care and seating them in a semicircle on his right hand. The twelve adopted an air of dignity at once and fixed their glances alternately upon the prisoner and the accuser.

"Now we're all met an' settled," said Bone, "it would be a shame if we kept the gents of this court away from their day's business. We'll get right down to the bottom of this at once. What's your name, Cap'n Foster?"

"My name is Malcolm Foster."

"Right you are. You, Chinaman, what are you called?"

"My name is Li Wo," he said.

As the Oriental spoke, his eye ran rapidly around the circle of faces that surrounded him, hunting for some sympathy, some trace of kindliness. But he could find none. All were merely half curious and half fierce except, on the farthest outskirts of the crowd, where stood a young fellow in the dress of a Mexican *vaquero*, his face shadowed by the enormous brim of his sombrero. This youth waited only for a moment, then turned and walked rapidly away toward the town.

Li Wo's heart bounded with hope, for he had recognized Ching in this familiar disguise. Something would be attempted in the way of rescue. Of that he could be sure. And for the moment he almost forgave the boy for his flirtation with a white girl that he had overheard that very morning.

"Get those names wrote down in your mind, Masters," instructed Jim Bone. "Now, Captain, suppose you tell us what you got ag'in' Li Wo?"

Captain Foster answered: "The other night, at Slater's Crossing, a man entered the hotel and attacked one of my men, Tim Dodd. Perhaps you had better hear the story from his own lips?"

"We got no terrible lot of time," said Jim Bone, "but we'll hear that story. Speak up, Dodd."

Dodd, adjusting the bandage that surrounded his head, advanced to the center of the circle and there made his speech in a gruff, deep voice, concluding with the assailant's announcement that he was striking in vengeance for Wei Sung.

This narrative was listened to with breathless interest. When it ended, Jim Bone remarked: "A cat can handle a dog ten times his weight, an' more. An' I figger some men are that way. I've heard of a bartender down at Monterey that got careless with this here Delancey an' was throwed through his own mirror behind his own bar. A mean customer to get cornered with is this here Delancey, an' they ain't no mistake. Go on, Captain."

Said big Captain Foster: "I want to explain that name . . . Wei Sung. In order to do this, I must go back a distance. I must go back over twenty years to a time when I sailed from China as master of a ship bound for Honolulu and then on to pick up a cargo of hides on the California coast. My wife, who was about to give birth to a child, sailed with me."

He paused, and then continued in a lower voice, so that all leaned a little forward to hear him.

"This is a painful subject to me, my friends. I shall deal with it as quickly as possible.

"The ship which I commanded had been fitted up with a number of passenger cabins, and these were almost entirely empty. But just before we sailed a young Chinaman came and begged to take one of them. He offered a good price, and I felt it was my duty to my owners to accept it, so he was brought aboard with his wife, who, like Missus Foster, was expecting a child. This Chinaman was Li Wo.

"The voyage was a very easy one, but when we were a week from Hawaii, my first mate missed a string of pearls from his strong box. Practically his entire profits from trading and working for years in the East had been invested in that string of pearls, so he became very excited. He at once suspected Li Wo and insisted on searching that cabin.

"This was done. Nothing suspicious was found,

except that under an edge of the rug in the cabin was a single pearl.

"My mate, in a fury, swore it was one of his string. I was angry, too, and ordered Li Wo to tell where he had hidden the rest of the pearls. He denied having touched them. He said the mate himself must have placed the pearl under the edge of the rug to put suspicion upon him, and therefore he knew nothing. I began to suspect the Chinaman as I listened to him. He was too cool and oily in his talk. An honest man is nearly always alarmed when he's accused wrongly. But a criminal knows how to pass off difficult situations.

"At any rate, I determined on a strong step. I threatened Li Wo with flogging, and, when he still refused to talk, I had him flogged by the third mate.

"The Chinaman was very stubborn. He fainted without having spoken. I was about to give up the job, and began to think he was innocent after all. However, as he recovered, the first mate rushed at him and ordered him triced up for another taste of the whip.

"That was too much for Li Wo. He broke down and confessed he had stolen the pearls and would show us where they were hidden . . . which was inside a false bottom of his chest. All the pearls were there in a wrapping of silk, and the first mate took them back.

"I thought the matter would drop there. The mate agreed with me that Li Wo had had enough punishment from the flogging. Besides, just before he landed, enough sorrow came both to Li Wo and to me to make me forget smaller grudges.

"We ran into a spell of rough weather just outside of Honolulu harbor, and both Li's wife and mine gave birth to children. The doctor remained a little too long working over my wife, perhaps. At any rate, he got to Li Wo's wife too late. She was dead, and the baby already born.

"My friends, this was a sad thing. Both the doctor and I felt it. And then another tragedy came to me as we entered Honolulu port. My baby son was dead."

XXVI

When Captain Foster paused at this point, there was not a murmur from the listening crowd, and every man looked down to the ground. They had come cheerfully to help preside at the hanging of a Chinaman, but they found a tragic tale of such a depth revealed that they were abashed and uneasy.

If it had been callously recited, it would not have disturbed them, but Captain Foster talked slowly, like one who seeks how he can state things in the simplest manner rather than as one who tries to make his points.

Foster went on: "It was a hard time, my friends. And what was hardest of all for me was that when we reached shore, and my poor wife recovered from the half delirium in which she had lain for a long time, to see the body of our boy prepared for burial, she declared that it was not hers, but the true baby had been stolen from her.

"If anything were needed to make this horrible

184

voyage sink into my mind, it was that. The illusion persisted, and she did not live to see the coast of California. She died, assuring me that we had been robbed. And I was unable to prove to her sufficiently that this could not have taken place.

"I beg your pardon for introducing such a subject. My only reason for doing so is to try to make you understand that there is no wish in me to recall that unhappy time. As for Li Wo and his stealing of the pearls, I should have been glad to forget him, and certainly I was not callous enough to prefer against him any charges of theft when he reached port. He had been doubly punished by the flogging and the death of his wife.

"But they say on the China coast that a Chinaman never forgets, and now I have reason to agree with them. The man who attacked Tim Dodd called out the name of Wei Sung, in whose name he had come for revenge. And now, gentlemen, I must give you the reason why I seized Li Wo when I met him in the street of San Salvadore a few minutes ago. Wei Sung was the name of his wife.

"Why he should have blamed me for her death I cannot tell, unless it was because the ship's doctor, who was employed with my own wife and child, was slow in coming to poor Wei Sung. He may have thought that this was done by my orders, whereas I had nothing to do with it. Or he may have held the flogging against me to such a degree that he was willing to hire a murderer to act against me here in California."

The accuser made a brief gesture.

"That is all I have to say, except that I have no malice against Li Wo. I am sorry for the troubles that came to him aboard my ship. I would be best pleased if he never had recalled the past to me, but since he has put a trained fighter on my heels to kill me if possible, it is necessary to strike back in some manner."

He stepped back and waited gravely for cross-examination.

"You've heard the man speak," said Jim Bone, after a proper interval. "Any questions?"

The jury shook their heads.

"Li Wo," demanded Jim Bone, "what have you got to say?"

Li Wo looked grimly at judge and jury, then turned to Foster.

"You flogged me on board your ship, Captain Foster?"

"I did," said the captain.

"You say that you found the pearls under my rug?"

"I found one pearl there."

"And the rest in my chest?"

"Yes."

"When my wife and I came on board the ship, the first mate tried to make me pay him extra money, and promised he would make my passage comfortable if I paid him. Otherwise, he said, he would put me in torment. I would not pay, and he arranged the rest. Who found that one pearl under the rug in my cabin? Please tell me."

"The first mate," said the captain with a sudden start.

"Who accused me of being the thief in the first place?"

"The mate," agreed the captain.

"And when I recovered from a fainting fit during the flogging, who rushed up and leaned over me?"

"The mate." Foster nodded.

"What he said to me," Li Wo testified impressively, "was that unless I spoke then, I should be flogged again, and, if I admitted that the pearls were in the false bottom of my chest, he would himself pretend to get them there . . . having them in his hand all the while. And who was it, Captain Foster, who found the pearls in my chest?"

"It was the mate."

"What became of this mate afterward?"

"He went bad," said Malcolm Foster slowly but honestly. "He turned into such a brute that I discharged him when we completed that voyage to New York."

"And finally?" asked Li Wo with a venomous politeness.

"He was killed in a drunken brawl . . . in New York's Chinatown, I believe."

Li Wo turned to the judge and the jury.

"You all know of Harry Delancey. Do you think I have enough money to hire him? Is he the sort of a man who would be hired out for murder?"

Jim Bone stirred uneasily.

"Now dog-gone' my spots," he said, "that's a pretty true thing. Handsome Harry is a wild young devil, but

I wouldn't ever say he's a cut-throat. Nobody knows of him ever doin' a thing in the dark like this. He takes his money where he finds it, but they ain't any record of him findin' it with a murder before. China money at that."

He paused, in doubt, and a juryman broke in: "What happened to the tenderfoot, Linton, when him and his girl were tackled by crooks in the hills? Who brought them through? What money was there in the job? Why, Handsome Harry done that job, as we all might well know. That ain't the kind of a man to take Chinese money for a murder in the dark."

Another man of the jury added with a snap: "Gents, look it here. Is they any doubt about what happened to this here man Dodd at Slater's Crossing?"

"They ain't no doubt," said Bone.

"Was the gent that done it followed, an' his gray hoss seen?"

"That happened, too."

"Was it Delancey?"

"They all say it was."

The juryman snarled abruptly, vindictively: "If you think that guy ain't the kind of chink to want to have a murder done, look at his face!"

The jury turned their heads upon Li Wo, and, although he made a sudden effort to compose his features, he could not prevent them from seeing malice there.

Jim Bone called out briskly: "Order, order! Is they anything more to be said?"

There was no answer.

"Then it appears to me like we had oughta take a vote. I ain't gonna tell you what I think about this here case, because it looks to me as plain as the nose on your face. You gents that think Li Wo is guilty, stand up on your hind laigs."

Every man of the jury rose instantly to his feet.

XXVII

Ching Wo, having made sure what the vigilantes were about, had gone straight back into San Salvadore. His skin was very dark, from a liberal use of walnut juice, and his upper lip was graced with a short, sparse, bristling mustache.

He walked straight up Main Street to the point where he had left his stallion, which he led down an alley and tethered it at the far end. Then he strolled over to the jail.

On the front steps of this sturdy little building sat Sheriff Wilson, whittling at a stick and chewing an enormous cud of tobacco.

Ching Wo raised his hat with ceremony. "I give you news, *señor*." He leaned forward a little and softened his voice to a whisper. "News of Handsome Harry."

The sheriff, with one keen glance, rose suddenly.

"Foller me, *amigo*," he said, and led the way up the jail steps, and into the jail to the little room reserved for him.

Sitting on the edge of his desk in his office, and

staring at the boy, Wilson exclaimed: "Kid, whatever you have to say, spill it out. An' if you can give me a lead, I'm your friend. Un'erstand? Your friend for keeps!"

He spoke solemnly, and the other bowed again, hat in hand.

"*Señor*," said Ching, "I can tell you where Delancey is right now."

"You can? Where, then?"

"Here in San Salvadore."

"The damn' impertinent rat!" roared the sheriff. "Can you lead me to him, son?"

"*Señor*, I do not need to lead. He is now in this room."

The good sheriff stared helplessly at his informant, and then groaned. "By the eternal Jehoshaphat!"

He did not move toward a gun, for Ching's arms were now lightly folded across his breast, and the sheriff could guess that either hand was now gripping the handle of a Colt revolver.

Lefty was a brave enough fighter, but he was no artist with weapons such as Handsome Harry had proved himself to be.

"Delancey," he said huskily, "what'll you have? What's on your mind?"

"I've come here," Ching replied, "to give you an opportunity to become famous."

"Thanks." Lefty sneered. "How'm I gonna get famous?"

"By jailing me, Wilson."

The sheriff drew a breath. "I don't foller this kind of jokin'."

"There's no joke. I'm willing to give myself in exchange for another man."

"Meanin' what?"

"Down the river they're holding court, under the judgment tree, you know."

"Damn them!" roared the sheriff. "Ain't I law enough for 'em? It's the blockhead Jim Bone that's carryin' on again!"

"It's Jim Bone," said the boy. "What will you do about it?"

"Who've they got?"

"A Chinaman named Li Wo."

"That old snake from Buffalo Flat? Aw, let him hang! It'll do nothin' but clear the air, from my way of thinkin'." He relaxed as he spoke. "What's a chink or two between friends, Delancey? An' what's that got to do with . . . ?"

"Go down to the oak tree, Lefty," urged Ching. "Scatter 'em . . . bring Li Wo through, safe and sound. If they have law to use against him, let them use it. But no lynch law, Lefty."

"What have you to do with Li Wo?" asked the sheriff.

"He's a friend of mine," said Ching.

The sheriff stared again. "Is it straight that you tried to kill Foster?"

"It's straight. And I did it because of what Li Wo told me. And I'll try it again if I have a chance. That brute, Foster, caused the death of poor Li Wo's wife."

Wilson was amazed. "You got me beat, Harry. Of all the gents I ever met, you're the outbeatin'est. I don't hardly dare to say what I guess this here visit of yours means."

"It means this, Wilson. Go down there and drag the Chinaman away from them, and I'm your man."

"You'll let me jail you, you mean?"

"I mean that."

"An' you want Li Wo jailed, too, instead of bein' lynched?"

Ching shook his head. "No, my story will clear him altogether. He didn't pay me a penny for attacking Foster, like Foster claimed. I went on my own hook because Li's story convinced me that Foster needed a trip to the cemetery."

The sheriff nodded. "I go down with you an' get Li Wo away from the crowd . . . then you promise to come back an' let me jail you?"

"That's it. Can you trust me, Lefty?"

Wilson stretched out his hand and it closed over the strong, slender fingers of Ching Wo. "It's a go, Delancey."

"Then start quickly!" urged Ching. "We haven't much time."

The sheriff shoved his hat down lower over his eyes, seized an extra gun from the wall, and rushed from the jail with Ching Wo at his side.

XXVIII

Two saddled horses stood before the jail. Upon them the pair threw themselves and rode furiously until they came within view of the judgment tree.

There Ching held up one hand and halted the wild gallop, for, as he pointed out, if they came with too much noise, the vigilantes were as apt as not to put a bullet through their captive's head and scatter with no more ado. So they went on at a mild jog of their horses and were able to come up unobserved to the outskirts of the crowd.

The crucial moment had come.

Poised upon a rock, some four or five feet off the ground, Li Wo stood with his hands still firmly lashed around him and a noose running from his neck over the limb of the tree. Jim Bone, in position before him, was going through with the final details of the regular ceremony.

"Li Wo, is they anything you want that we can give you?"

The yellow face of Li Wo puckered, but he said not a word.

"Failin' of wantin' anything . . . say a drink, now? Is they anything you wanna say to us, Li?" went on Bone persuasively. "You might figger," he continued, like a good host who wishes to cheer the departed, "that you're about to barge off on a tolerable long journey, an' they's a good deal of doubt about where you're gonna wind up with it. Now, if they's any little directions you'd like to leave with us all, an' messages, an' such-like things, we'll write 'em down an' deliver 'em, free of charge."

Li Wo's upper lip merely lifted and rage glittered in his eyes. That was all. Never had a prisoner in the hands of the vigilantes showed less terror.

"It's come to this here point," said Jim Bone, "that we gotta put an end to the job. We can't linger it out no more, because a lot of these gents are busy an' they've carved a big chunk out of their time for you, Li Wo. I'll wind up by merely sayin' you'll get a good, decent Christian burial. An' if that means anything to your heathen soul, good bye, Li Wo, an' a happy trip for you."

Li Wo, for answer, broke into a strange laughter. It did not sound like the mirth of a white man. There was a crow and a cackle of fierce joy in it, and mockery that chilled the blood of all men present.

Instinctively the vigilante chief turned about to follow the direction of Li Wo's glance. Thus he saw a most unwelcome sight. The sheriff was upon them.

It was the accepted rule that the sheriff should take the activities of the vigilantes as reinforcing and supplementing his own, but Lefty Wilson looked far from passive at this moment. He carried in his hands a big caliber double-barreled shotgun, loaded with small shot, scraps of iron, and mischief of all descriptions. Just beside him rode a wiry young Mexican with a similar weapon in his hands. If that pair of guns were

194

fired upon the crowd, they looked capable of ripping away many faces.

As Jim Bone's jaw fell, the rest of the assembled gang looked in the same direction and saw the same thing. Only one group stood fast, and these were the men grasping the rope attached to Li Wo.

A brawny miner yelled: "Let's finish the chink in spite of Lefty Wilson. Give a heave, lads!"

Instantly Li Wo was plucked above the rock and left gasping and kicking upon the empty air, doing the strange dance of death that old-time Westerners loved to see. But he descended instantly, for Ching Wo, with a shriek of rage and of horror, had charged his horse in among the hangmen.

El Rey was a savage animal. Straight through the line he bolted. One man was hurled a dozen yards off and lay, gasping and groaning, with broken ribs and no wind whatever. Two more were knocked down. A third was trampled and broken under the ruthless hoofs of the stallion. However, the third had the wonderful luck to escape without any serious injury; he jumped up and fled with a screech.

There was no resistance. The sight of the ruin of the line of hangmen had a great effect upon the crowd.

The leveled shotguns did the rest, and with a yell the mob turned and bolted, Jim Bone rushing through the rest with tremendous leaps, like the spry hops of a jack rabbit. It was no longer tragedy, but broadest farce.

Soon the two rescuers were left alone, with the groaning man who had been shouldered by the horse, and Li Wo himself. The latter was already up. The rope was loosed from around his neck and his hands freed by a touch of Ching's knife.

"Father," said the boy quietly in a shaken voice, "I give praise to all the bright ones who watch over you."

Li Wo turned to the sheriff and bowed deeply.

"All that is done by just men for poor Chinamen is not forgotten, Mister Wilson," he said. "May. . . ."

The sheriff cut in rudely: "You got a stretched neck, but a living one, Li Wo. You better run out of here as fast as you can before the boys come back for you. In the meantime, you can thank God that you once did a good turn for Handsome Harry Delancey."

Li waved his hand.

"Git!" ordered Lefty Wilson.

And Li Wo got with speed. Only once he turned around to view with wonder and a shaken head the sight of Ching Wo riding off, side-by-side, with the sheriff.

Li headed straight down the valley, but this sight meant so much that he could not contain himself.

The wily old Chinaman knew, as the sheriff had said, that it would be safer for him to vanish from the town of San Salvadore and not come back until another six months had filled the streets with a new generation of gold seekers and idlers. But curiosity got the better of caution, so he turned back toward the town.

Skulking from tree to tree, he entered San Salvadore from the rear, where the hills slanted down toward Chinatown. Almost at once he came into a narrow alley.

A porter was carrying a great load, bowed under the carrying pole, from which a huge basket was suspended at either end. Li Wo passed without a word, but next encountered an Oriental in silk, with softly shod feet. He knew that man, but the latter produced a fan from up his sleeve and held it before his face.

It was the Chinese sign that the wielder of the fan was very busy and, not intending any discourtesy, wished to go on without greeting the other. But Li Wo was too excited to regard this signal. He touched the sleeve of the other, who stopped unwillingly.

"Sun Chee," said Li, speaking in Chinese, "if you are hurrying on your way, tarry a moment, still, because I am distressed. I am in great trouble and danger. Let me go with you to your house."

Sun Chee's eyes flickered up and down the street. Then he clutched the arm of the other, dragging him into the first doorway.

There he answered: "We know what has nearly happened down by the river. But that cannot happen every day. You cannot have enough money to keep on buying white men to give up their lives for you."

"What white men have died for me?" asked Li Wo eagerly.

"Is not Mister Harry Delancey in the jail for you?" retorted Sun Chee.

"He? Is he in the jail?" inquired Li Wo, biting his lip.

"He is. Men say he has given himself up to pay the price for your life, Li Wo. Well, well, it is like some story of China's golden age. Sons in those days would die for their fathers, but in these times they have forgotten the old virtues. Do you hear me, Li Wo? You, too, have a son. Have you taught him to do as much for you as this white man has been taught to do by your money?"

He asked it half spitefully and half in plain curiosity. Li Wo, feeling that the man had stepped perilously close to the truth, merely answered: "This Delancey is one honest man among all the Americans. Because I have been able to give him kindnesses, not because of money, he has helped me. But is it possible that this good man is now in jail?"

"They stand in line to go past him and look at his face where he sits behind the bars," returned Sun Chee.

Li Wo blinked, remembering certain arts that had been taught to Ching Wo before which the strongest locks dissolved and left a prisoner free. This trust was rudely shocked when Sun Chee added: "They have handcuffed a strong fellow to him with irons, so that Mister Delancey cannot escape without taking the other with him, and that is hardly possible."

Li Wo stared with a sudden helplessness out the shadow of the doorway at the keen mountain sun that blazed along the narrow street.

Sun Chee made a little gesture. "And now I must go on. I am a busy man. You, I believe, were walking up the street?"

Li Wo took the broad hint and departed. His friend went the other way.

XXIX

The ravine where Stephen Linton had staked out his claim *hummed* with many voices and *clanged* with the noise of hammers. A thousand men swarmed through it; everywhere they were knocking chips from rocks, as though they expected that the blow of a hammer might reveal naked virgin gold within.

Often they turned hungry eyes upon Linton's claim. That stretch of rocks also was alive with men, but Linton's laborers were working systematically, lethargically. They were the hired hands, bitterly taking their days' wages to dig gold for another man.

Linton had struck it rich. Right now he was not paying any attention to the swarms of workers. He was busy with a tall, bald-headed, hook-nosed attorney named Bentley, who sat with him on a rock before the tent, his hat on the ground beside him, talking earnestly.

The attorney was summing up: "Your idea, Linton, is that money is no object, and it must flow like water to get this young rascal, Delancey, out of trouble. Is that right?"

"Exactly."

"You're impatient," said Bentley.

Linton answered quickly: "Of course, I'm impatient. We're in a lawless place. How can I tell when a crowd may rise in the street and storm the jail and take that boy out on a lynching party, such as they organized for the Chinaman?"

Margery Linton came suddenly to the door of the tent and stood breathless, listening.

"Go back to your work, Margery," said her father briskly. "I'm going to handle this affair. You can't do a thing about it, as you should be able to see for yourself."

She did not stir.

"There's no great hatred of the boy around here," Linton went on. "Nine out of ten are his friends. Everyone speaks favorably, for instance, about the way he brought Margery and me through the hands of the Saunders gang. They speak even more favorably of his insane chivalry in jeopardizing his life to save the Chinaman. You couldn't get a jury here to convict him."

"No doubt you're right. But the fact is, Linton, they've planned to take him away to San Francisco."

"Take him away?"

The lawyer nodded. "Yeah."

"Then he'll stand a good chance of being hanged in Frisco?"

"The brightest chance in the world."

"What will they charge against him?" Linton inquired anxiously.

"Murderous assault on Tim Dodd," the lawyer replied.

"But Tim Dodd is still alive?"

"Of course he is. But you see what this shows about Delancey? That he'd never pause to think twice in attacking any man with intent to kill."

"But Delancey didn't kill . . . that kid stopped his hand when the light showed he was at the wrong man."

"Nobody doubts," said Bentley patiently, "that the boy is a good, clean fighter. But the fact is . . . he made that attack."

"Walk down the hill," suggested Linton. "I'll go halfway back to the town with you. We've got to work it out."

As they started down, Margery Linton sprang up from the rock on which she had sunk down and would have run after them had not a shadow slipped across the ground in front of her.

The girl found herself looking into the yellow face of a Chinaman. She did not speak; the apparition had almost startled her first thought from her mind, when the other said: "They never will free Harry Delancey. Only you can do that."

He held up before her eyes a little red phial.

"You will go to see him, because your heart is gentle and good. Men know that you owe him kindness, and they will not be surprised if you take him a little bunch of flowers. Among the stems conceal this. It will save him . . . it will set him free."

He paused, then added simply: "I am the man for whom he is about to die. I am Li Wo."

XXX

On a drowsy afternoon Captain Foster walked down the main street of San Salvadore with an escort of two sailors. Since the adventure in the hotel at Slater's Crossing, all three had developed the eyes of hawks. They were armed and ready for trouble.

Thus Foster strolled along the winding highway and entered the jail, leaving his two sailors at the door. He found Sheriff Lefty Wilson within. The latter nodded and smiled at him.

"I've come to tell you," said Captain Foster, "it was not my suggestion that made the crowd take Li Wo to the judgment tree and prepare to hang him. I was following, as I took it to be, the custom of the country."

"A dog-gone' good custom, now an' then," remarked the sheriff amiably. "I don't hold nothin' ag'in' you, Cap'n Foster. Set down an' rest your feet."

"I want to see young Delancey," said the captain, "if that's possible."

"It's after visitin' hours," was the answer, "but you're a different case. Maybe you've got a thing or two to ask him, eh?"

Straightway he led Foster to the boy's cell. There were four other cells, and every one was full. In each one of those four the occupant was lying on his couch, sleeping or pretending to sleep.

But in the cell of Handsome Harry a small lantern was burning, because of the darkness that pervaded the small-windowed jail. There sat the prisoner with a burly guard manacled to him. The guard's left hand was clasped with steel to the gunman's right wrist.

The guard was unarmed, for the very good reason that by some maneuver Delancey might gain possession of the weapon and thereby master the guard. But the guard himself had not the key of the lock of the manacle.

Everything that prudence could do to keep Harry Delancey under guard was done here, and at the first outcry of the guard two picked men would rush in, guns in hand. That was not all. Every four hours the manacled guard was released and another was given that partnership in bondage, so that there might be no relaxing of watchfulness.

Malcolm Foster came to the cell and looked in on the prisoner by the dingy light.

The guard waved his hand cheerfully at the sheriff. "All well an' restin' easy."

"That's what the rooster crowed before the fox bit his head off," warned the sheriff. "You have a hold on yourself, young feller, an' remember it's Handsome Harry you're guardin." He added to the prisoner: "Here's Cap'n Foster come to talk to you, Mister Delancey."

Captain Foster took note of that "mister". It was a most unusual term of courtesy in the West, brought in for strangers or for those held in the greatest respect.

Ching Wo looked straight at the visitor without saying a word.

Foster came to the point. "Delancey, will you tell me what sent you after me?"

Ching said nothing, but his eyes fixed steadily upon the skipper's face, reading every line of it, probing at his eyes, striving to find there the things that Li Wo had told him existed in this man's soul. But in spite of himself, Ching could not see them at all.

This was a sufficiently grim man of action, a stern, strong and purposeful leader of others, but the young captive did not find cruelty in Foster's expression. Therefore, he was baffled, although he strove to hide it.

Said the sheriff: "I might as well tell you that what you say now ain't goin' to be held ag'in' you at the trial, Delancey. You can talk out with a gent like the captain as though I wasn't here."

Ching smiled a little. Then he responded: "Captain Foster, why do you think I went to the hotel that night?"

"To find me," was the instant reply.

"Was there any reason why I should want to find you?"

"You spoke the name of Wei Sung."

At that, Ching's eyes closed somewhat, with an expression of tenderness.

Of this the captain took note and wondered at it.

"You came," said Foster, "to kill me, for the sake of what a Chinaman had told you about his wife. Is that correct?"

Ching did not answer.

"Come, come," urged the captain. "Is there any reason why we should not be candid with one another?"

Foster paused, and in the pause he scowled at the floor, but even then the boy did not see in the skipper's face the brutality for which he was hungrily watching.

"Delancey, I'm frankly bewildered. I don't see what there is about Li Wo to draw you so violently to his side."

"I can explain it," Ching replied at last. "If it were not for him, I should not be alive today."

Foster nodded slowly, as one who considers. "You owe him a great debt. You are paying it in a great way, Delancey. You move me to the heart."

Ching looked with new eyes at the speaker. But he had heard endless tales from Li Wo of the duplicity of the Occidental, his skill in lying and reckless truth-telling. The prisoner would not easily be drawn in.

"If you could let me at the bottom of the mystery," said Captain Foster, "I will make a promise. I will agree to give no testimony against you, and to with-hold the testimony of Tim Dodd, also."

"Easy there, Captain!" exclaimed the sheriff.

"You understand," went on Foster, "if we talk against you in San Francisco, it seems clear that you'll hang for that night's work at the Crossing?"

Ching was still silent.

"Will you tell me this . . . ? Did you ever serve on board any of my ships?"

Still the boy did not speak.

"Because," persisted the captain, "it seems to me that I remember your face, sadly, as though it were connected with some important event in my life. Can you tell me that much, Delancey, without committing yourself?"

Ching responded with a burst of scorn: "Why should I trust you, Captain Foster?"

The skipper looked at him with open eyes, as one puzzled. "My word isn't doubted by those who know me well."

The boy stared hard, and the longer he looked the more he felt the truth of this remark. Captain Foster might be harsh, but not a facile liar.

Then Ching cried out with a suddenly ringing voice, forgetful of the others, except the big sailor before him. For something drew him with a wonderful force toward this man—not the hatred that Li Wo had taught him, but sympathy and understanding.

"Foster, tell me truly . . . you caused the death of Wei Sung?"

The captain did not draw back. He took a short step forward and answered: "So help me God, I'm innocent of any wrong to that poor Chinese girl."

Bewildered and uncertain, Ching heard Foster's declaration. Then he shrugged his shoulders.

"Some liars are saved by their lies. You won't be one of them, Captain Foster."

"Not even my word, Delancey?" asked the visitor gloomily. He flushed a little and added with a strange humility: "Let me tell you, man, I've traded in a great many parts of the world, and my word has been worth money in all of them."

Ching made a graceful gesture, slowly, with one hand turned palm up. "I give you warning. They say the rattler is an honest snake because he gives warning."

Foster turned to the sheriff. "This fellow seems to be an inveterate rascal. You hear him threatening me in your own presence, my friend?"

"I hear him," answered the sheriff, nodding. "But that don't mean nothin'. He'll be hangin' by the neck in Frisco before long."

The skipper threw up both hands.

"I can't understand it. And mind you, Delancey," he went on, "the sheriff will forgive the offer I made to you a moment ago. Tell me your secret . . . because a secret there must be . . . and I'll use all my power to get you free."

Ching forced a grin. He did not need to make any other reply, for Foster turned abruptly away. Halfway down the aisle with the sheriff, he paused again and looked back. Then he went slowly on, as though his wish still drew him back to the prisoner.

XXXI

It was growing dusk when the second visitor arrived after hours. Margery Linton came down the aisle with the sheriff.

"I gotta go along," he said. "The idea is, Miss

Linton, you an' your father have reason to be pretty fond of this here Delancey. I don't wish him no harm, but I can't let things be passed inta him."

"There's only this bunch of wildflowers," the girl explained. "I thought they might make his place a little more cheerful."

"Sure, sure," agreed Lefty Wilson. "Lemme have 'em. I'll give 'em to him, an' welcome. He can put 'em in the water basin if he wants to."

They came before the cell. Ching stood up. His dark eyes gleamed once, then grew blank.

"My father sent me," said the girl. "He wants to know if there is anything we can do for you. Can we send you in fruit or some extra fare of any sort?"

"The sheriff is very good to all of his prisoners," answered Ching. "There's nothing I need. But your kindness . . . I thank you for that."

"Our kindness?" returned Margery, with a break in her voice. "We've found a good lawyer to fight for you, Harry. He'll bring you off, if possible."

"If such a man can open the door for me," said Ching, "then I'll owe you as much as my life is worth, Margery."

The sheriff passed in the flowers. "Here's something to buck you up, Delancey."

Ching raised them to his face. "They are very fragrant."

His fingers, working subtly among the bound stems, touched the hard, cold surface of a glass phial, whereupon he lowered the blossoms and smiled at the girl.

"They smell like the free open country to me," he said. "There's a scent of wild honey in them."

After a brief pause Lefty Wilson had to close the jail for the night, so he excused himself for asking Miss Linton to close the interview. She bade good bye, clinging an instant to the bars of the cell, her eyes filling with tears.

Ching bowed deeply. As she went off, his glance followed, cherishing every step she took.

"What's the smell of wild honey like?" the guard asked curiously.

"It's something that can't be explained," was the reply. "The point is, only one sort of men can understand it."

"What sort of men?"

Ching waited a moment. "Starving men," he said at last. "Men dying of hunger, my friend."

The other swore. "Look here, Delancey, are you moonstruck or just plain nutty?"

"Did you ever find wild honey when you were sick with hunger?" Ching wanted to know.

The guard scratched his head. "I dunno as I ever did. I would rather've found fried bacon, for my part."

"You would," said Ching. "And you're quite right, too. Things that are too sweet have poison in 'em. Better leave the honey for the bees that make it."

The guard looked askance at his companion, and then remarked: "You'll be needin' all yer strength. Why not turn in an' try to sleep."

"Sleep?" echoed Ching. "Certainly. A very good idea."

He had drawn out the phial from the flowers and managed to glance down at its reddish contents. The instant he saw it, the faintest of smiles touched his lips. Dextrously he removed the cap of the phial. Then, pretending to smell the bouquet, he managed to sprinkle some of the red fluid upon the blossoms. At once a thin, rather acridly sweet fragrance filled the air.

"What's that?" inquired the guard, sniffing.

"What?" returned the prisoner.

"Don't you smell nothin'?"

"Oh, you mean the *somnos?*" asked Ching.

"The . . . what?"

"These little red flowers. *Somnos.*"

The guard stared. "That's a funny name."

"It means sleep," said Ching. "The smell of 'em is a great cure for insomnia."

"The hell it is!"

"Why, it would make you dizzy almost with one whiff."

"*Bah!*" sneered the guard. "Lemme try."

He raised the bouquet to his face and breathed deeply. The result made him sag back with a grunt of surprise.

"What the devil's in these flowers? Dog-gone if I ain't dizzy."

He breathed in from the flowers deeply again, then lay half stupefied, muttering: "Funny . . . never heard of 'em before."

"No. Only the Indians know about them," said

Ching. "They . . . and the Chinese," he added cautiously, but vindictively.

As the guard's eyes were closed, Ching carefully sprinkled some more drops upon the broad bosom of the man of the law.

"Seems to be gettin' into my head," murmured the other drowsily. "Mountin' right up into my brain. I . . . *aw*. . . ."

And his breathing became regular. The instant this happened, Ching redoubled the application upon his companion's breast. The guard relaxed in every muscle and lay unconscious.

Ching's head was ringing, although he had not inhaled a 100th part of the odor taken by his companion.

However, he doubled in the palm of his right hand. It allowed him to slip easily from the handcuff, and, being free, he stole across to the farther side of the cell and there drew in a great breath of pure air. It steadied him, and prepared him for what he had now to perform.

XXXII

They had searched Ching from head to foot. But they had not suspected his long black curls of being a wig. This he moved a trifle and drew from beneath it several of those minute steel blades with which he had been taught to read the mind of the most intricate lock.

Armed with these, the prisoner crouched beside the

door and, reaching through, started to work. The lock was very big and partially stuck with rust, so much so that it always *screeched* whenever the jailer's key was applied.

Just as Ching made this discovery, the sound of footsteps and the sight of a lantern swinging down the aisle warned him to get back to the cot. He barely had laid down again at the side of the unconscious guard when Sheriff Wilson and a stranger stood at the door of the cell.

"Hello, there," greeted the sheriff.

The guard did not stir. Ching merely groaned, as though painfully overcome with sleep.

"Look at 'em," said the stranger. "Dead to the world. That Delancey ain't no more than a boy, is he?"

"No more than a boy, by the look of him. More than a hundred boys by the hell he raises. I don't wish him no harm, though."

"What's the smell in the air?"

"I don't smell nothin'. I got a cold."

"Well, it's somethin' makes me dizzy."

"What've you had to drink this afternoon?"

"Hardly more than a drop."

"A couple of your drops would fill a bucket. Come along, old son. Let's vamoose out of here before you get so dizzy your head spins around."

They went off, the lantern making the shadows of the bars sweep in a crazy and entangled pattern upon the walls and the ceiling.

Hardly were they gone before Ching was at the door

once more. The lock bolt shuddered and finally yielded with a distinct groan. Ching stepped into the passage, closing the door of the cell behind him. He delayed only an instant at the lock of the outer door, opened it, and stepped into the welcome darkness.

For a little while Ching, against the wall, breathed deeply to free his lungs from the poisonous fumes. So greatly was he affected that he thought with some concern of the quantity of the drug that his guard had inhaled. Then he passed around the side of the jail until he came beneath the office window.

Kicking off the oversize shoes that had been given to him and shedding his coat, the fugitive climbed almost naked up to the window ledge and peered in.

There he saw the sheriff not three feet from the window, sitting in a chair with his side turned toward it somewhat, and yet facing it sufficiently for his heels to be cocked upon the sill. The good sheriff was smoking a cigar with the slow enjoyment of a connoisseur.

Ching Wo gathered himself as a cat gathers for a spring.

In *jujitsu* there is nothing so important as to learn how to handle one's self when in an awkward position. He who is thrown must be able to fall lightly and roll to his feet. Or if he falls on his side heavily, he must know how to gain all fours and leap again, like a beast of prey.

Ching stealthily prepared himself at the narrow ledge of the window, worked his way over the window ledge, and doubled his knees.

The sheriff opened his eyes wide. He saw before him the face of Harry Delancey; he saw a slender, half naked body, covered with whipcord muscles. Then, before he could shout, this creature sprang at him and caught his throat in the crook of its elbow.

The sheriff went over with a *crash*; his head *clicked* against the floor. It seemed to Wilson that he was unconscious for only a moment, but when he sat up again, dizzily supporting himself with both hands spread out upon the floor, he saw Delancey seated upon the edge of the desk.

The escaped prisoner was swinging one leg and regarding the sheriff with rather amused eyes, like one watching a show.

Ching was now wearing the same Mexican clothes that he had worn on entering the jail. About his hips appeared the same gaudy sash. The same broad sombrero shadowed his face. But a gun on the desk face beside him belonged to the sheriff.

Ching was rolling a cigarette. This he finished making, then lighted it with a match that he snapped into the air. With fascinated eyes the sheriff followed its flight by the thin streak of bluish smoke. He noted the faint scent of sulphur.

He was noticing, in fact, all details—the slenderness of Delancey's foot, the highness of his heel, the very pull of the cloth over his knee, as his foot swung back and forth. Men on their way to death—the last mile—notice details with the same minuteness. Lefty Wilson felt his final moment had come.

XXXIII

Recovering from his daze, Sheriff Lefty Wilson sized up the situation and decided his last moment had come. But he was not afraid.

"What's the verdict?" he growled.

"I hope you're feeling better," said Ching.

"I am," grunted the sheriff. He rose and faced Ching without flinching.

"I wanted to have a little chat with you before I left," the boy explained.

The sheriff nodded. His eyes went quickly to the door and window. After measuring chances, he decided they were worthless. He could not escape from this slender devil, who was swifter than a cat's paw in his movements.

"First of all," said Ching, "I believe you are wearing two shirts. I need one of them. You see, I am less likely to be recognized if I walk out in your checked shirt."

Wilson complied with the request. "Well, what next?"

"I think this game has gone far enough," the youth announced. "I don't mind being tagged a few times, but. . . ."

"I ain't been houndin' you, Delancey," interrupted the sheriff. "You come in an' give yourself up to me this time. You made a fair bargain out of it."

"I remembered that when I came at you through the window," commented Ching. "Otherwise, I had intended to kill you."

Lefty Wilson swallowed hard.

"Now," went on Ching, "suppose we look at the thing fairly and squarely, as you say. You've had in your hands a young Chinese boy, a friend of mine."

"I played easy with him," insisted the sheriff. "I never bothered him after you took him outta jail."

Ching raised a hand, protesting against such interruption.

"In the second place," he said, "you've had me, in person, in your hands. This isn't desirable, from my viewpoint. You threaten to spoil my morale. The effect I have on the rest of the world, in short. And I think you ought to agree to leave my trail, don't you?"

"Otherwise?" inquired the sheriff.

Ching softly touched the revolver. "We won't go into details. But what would you say of a young and high-spirited sheriff who committed suicide with his own revolver because a valuable prisoner had escaped?"

At this Lefty Wilson stiffened and drew up. Then he said through tight lips: "You've got the upper hand, young feller. You can drill me clean, but, so long as I've got a spark of life in me, I'm gonna stick to your trail."

Ching listened thoughtfully. At last he picked up the sheriff's revolver, juggled it for a moment, then tossed it aside.

"Will you give me five minutes before you sound an alarm, or shall I stay here and tie and gag you first?"

"I'll give you five minutes," replied the sheriff,

ashen-faced with shame. He groaned as he watched Ching slide through the window.

Dropping to the ground, the fugitive gave one swift glance around, then walked rapidly up the alley to the main street. This he crossed through a swarming crowd, just as an outburst of shouting came from the jail.

Ching went on down another alley, and presently found himself in the twisted tangle of the Chinese quarter. He knew what house to try, and, finding two Chinamen squatting in the doorway, he made a sign. They drew aside and let him into a dark, narrow corridor, stale with tobacco smoke.

Up this he passed to a winding flight of stairs and he climbed past two floors until he reached the flat roof of the house. There sat Li Wo on a mat, alone with his pipe.

Ching fell upon his knees, but did not speak. The older man removed the pipe from his mouth and said: "It is Ching."

"It is I, oh, my father," was the reply. Emotion choked the youth.

Li Wo, in the meantime, began to smoke again, puffing calmly toward the stars. Then he pointed across the roofs.

Far up the ravine they could see the tossing and crossing of many lights, dipping up and down among the rocks like boats in the water.

"They are still at work," he said.

Ching stared hard in that indicated direction, for he

knew it was Linton's claim, and these were hungry gold seekers struggling furiously to locate near the lucky man.

"The man is very rich," Li Wo continued. "He is rich now, and he will be richer hereafter. He will be loaded down with gold. He will be full of it. The dog of a white man takes out the treasures of the earth, but the Chinaman will have it in the end. Do you hear, Ching?"

"I hear," Ching answered doubtfully.

Li Wo again fell into an impressive silence. Plainly he was very much displeased with something. Ching was soon to find out why, although in no direct manner.

Suddenly his father broke out: "Have you found a woman, Ching?"

Ching sighed. He looked down at the dark shadow of the roof and up at the brightness of the stars, wishing heartily he were 1,000 miles from that spot.

"Answer!" commanded the father.

Ching said: "I have found a woman."

"That is very strange," commented Li Wo. "A wise son and a virtuous young man does not know what love of a woman is until his father has placed a bride before him. I have never done that."

"I came on her myself," Ching admitted miserably.

Suddenly the older man leaped to his feet and rushed at the boy. He caught him by the arm, and his sharp nails dug through the cloth and hurt the hard flesh.

"Go down to the street and stand there to say your prayers until I come down to you!" commanded Li Wo. "I must sit here alone and ask the gods if they have given me a blessing or a curse in such a son."

Ching Wo was on his way down the stairs when a burly form arose before him, ascending, and he recognized Fow Ming, attended by two servants. Ching slipped behind them, for he guessed that this was something he would need to overhear.

When they reached the roof, he lingered close to the trap door, and there he was able to hear clearly all that passed. Fow Ming was already in the midst of an excited oration. He had found his daughter. He had sent her safely escorted back to San Francisco. And he had discovered that Ching was responsible for the kidnapping.

These facts Fow Ming communicated to Li Wo, the proposed father-in-law of his daughter.

After that Ching heard shuffling slippers as his father hurried up and down the roof. Then he slunk down to the street and waited.

It was a vigil that lasted more than an hour before Fow Ming rushed out from the house and went down the street with his attendants. Li Wo came shortly afterward. He hurried to the nearest alley mouth and turned into this. Ching followed, and there among the thick shadows confronted the older man.

Ching was glad there was no more light, for Li Wo's rage was terrible enough, being heard, without a glimpse of his contorted face.

"I have raised a son who is a sharp knife that cuts my throat," snarled Li Wo.

Ching did not speak, because to him the peril in which he stood was greater than that of one tottering above the brink of a vast precipice.

"There has been nothing in my life for twenty years except your welfare," said Li Wo. "I have poured everything into one dish, and see! The dish is broken . . . everything is spilled. I have worked and prayed and fasted, and all for an ungrateful son. I shall not call you a son, but a. . . ."

There was a deep groan of horror and fear from Ching. Instead of continuing, Li Wo pressed both his hands to his face and answered groan with groan.

"Do you know what Fow Ming has come to tell me?" he asked at last.

I know," the boy responded. "For what I have done, all the torments are not too much, continually applied all the rest of my life. I cannot tell you what it was that made me do the thing. Only, suddenly, I could not endure to marry her."

"Marry her you shall!" ordered Li Wo. "Marry her you shall, or else I will put such a curse on your head. . . ."

"I shall marry her," Ching Wo answered slowly.

"It was the face of the white woman that turned your heart," said Li Wo.

"Yes," admitted the boy. "It was that. Now that you say it, I know it is true. After looking at her, I could not think of the daughter of Fow Ming. But I see now that I have done wrong and committed a great sin. I have lied to you, and that lie is like lead, crushing my heart."

"There are these three things," said Li Wo. "You have not done as you should have done. Fow Ming's daughter is not your wife, you have sat at the feet of a white woman, and Captain Foster is still alive. Oh, Ching, your mother's spirit weeps over you."

"There are three things that I shall do," declared Ching Wo. "I shall marry the daughter of Fow Ming. I shall kill Captain Foster. And I shall see the white woman to say farewell to her forever."

"Yes," said Li Wo. "The hardest thing you leave to the last."

"Yes. It is the hardest. I could sit for a long time, silent, even in the room where she has been and gone away. That would be happiness to me."

Li Wo gripped his arm. "My poor son. I have been stern and harsh to you, but now I understand. There is a devil in that woman. Into what bodies do the devils slip easily except into the bodies of women? It is that devil that has tempted you to evil and done it with smiling and with beauty. A white woman's beauty is the beauty of hell. It will give you one moment of pleasure on earth and a thousand million years of fire in hell hereafter."

Ching Wo listened with a bowed head, like one who sacrifices before a god.

XXXIV

It was no sound, she was sure, that wakened Margery Linton in her room at the San Salvadore Hotel. For, since the mine was an assured success, her father was guarding it with armed men, and he could trust the girl to the security of the town.

The hour was almost dawn, and even the gamblers of San Salvadore had gone to bed. No wind whistled through the crannies and the crevices of the ramshackle place. No footfall *creaked* on the stairs up along the halls. No one snored like a nasal trumpet in any adjoining room. It was, in fact, the single hour of holy silence in San Salvadore, when it seemed as though Nature were holding its breath over the sins that the little town committed in the remaining twenty-three hours of the day.

But yet Margery found herself suddenly staring with wide eyes at the moonlight that drifted from the western window across the foot of her bed. It touched upon the back of a chair, and it threw upon the wall a still pattern of shadow from the overhanging branch of a pine tree outside the window.

It seemed to Margery that she had wakened from some delightful dream. Her heart was beating happily; she tried to drift back into it, but could not. Her eyes remained wide, and so she observed, although she heard not a sound, the opening of the door of her room.

Then she saw a slender fellow enter with a wonderfully easy and gliding step. He crossed the room to the center, where the moonlight fell upon his face. The girl's heart bounded again, for it was Handsome Harry Delancey.

The visitor was poised like a wild panther, looking quickly, eagerly into every corner.

He glided over to the maiden and leaned above her. Margery kept eyes closed and tried to breathe evenly, although it seemed to her that the effort would stifle her. Presently she felt that the weight of his nearness was removed, and, venturing a glance through her eyelashes, she saw him take from the hollow of his left arm a quantity of flowers.

Their fragrance stirred lightly about her as he laid them softly, one by one, about the bed. She could even note the pale gleam of his hands, and the thoughtful look in his face as he stepped back to consider his work.

When he had done, he went to the central table, took up pen and paper, and then she heard the faint *scratching* of pen upon paper.

What was he writing there?

Many things rushed through the girl's mind. Above all, the way they had galloped through the wood of the great pines with the way spotted with silver and black before them. Then she remembered how Captain Foster had talked to them the night before—Captain Foster returned from an adventure so strange that he would not speak much about it. Only, when he mentioned Handsome Harry Delancey, it was with deep, sincere emotion.

Her practical father had said: "Such a fellow, Captain Foster, properly handled, put into the right line of work, would make a name that the world would know about."

Margery had felt no sympathy with the idea. She knew what making a name meant. It consisted of laboring hard for twenty years. Marriage, children, and all human relationships except useful ones were reduced to the rank of sheer incident, while the toiler laid the foundation of his fame. Afterward he would have reputation. That meant headlines in the newspapers, visits from important and very dull people, a brownstone house in Boston or New York, and sometimes a stodgy tour as far as Paris.

Linton's daughter sighed a little. Still the pen kept *scratching*. Then Ching turned and laid a fold of paper on the bed among the flowers.

And suddenly she knew it was this strange man's way of saying farewell, so silently, in the middle heart of the night, with none to see or hear. She felt him lean above her, and knew his lips had touched her hair.

"I've been watching you, Harry," she said.

Ching started very slightly. A leveled gun would have disturbed him as much, but no more, she knew.

But he took off his hat and she could see the handsome profile of his face, looking like pale stone in the moonlight, stone delicately chiseled by an antique master.

"I've spoiled your sleep, then," he said.

"You're going away, Harry," she remarked softly.

"You've come to leave me flowers and a note. That's it, isn't it?"

"Yes," he responded. "If you watched me, you must have thought you were being decorated for burial, Margery."

"You're going off to do some other wild thing, Harry. You may as well confess that. You're going after Captain Foster again. Nothing will stop you the third time, I'm afraid."

"I hope," said Ching Wo, his voice saddening, "I never look upon his face again." He paused. "I'll never see you after tonight."

The maiden drew herself up in bed and pulled a dressing gown about her shoulders. She was trembling violently.

"It's the Chinese girl you told me of. You're following her?"

Ching paused, and, while Margery waited for the answer, a strong hand seemed to grip her throat. It choked her, and suddenly she had to breathe, he was silent for so long, and that breath was a sob.

Ching Wo came closer. "Do you care so, Margery?"

"Do you think I'm c-c-crying and m-making such a fool of myself for nothing?" she asked.

At this he moved still closer. All at once her stifled sobbing ended, for she could see misery in his face. She sat bolt upright, gripping the edge of the bed, and the moon turning the round of her arm into translucent marble.

"Oh, Harry, Harry," she said, "it's hard for you to

leave me, too. It's not all the Chinese girl that's in your heart. You care a little for me, too. Will you say that?"

"Suppose there were no Chinese girl," he suggested. "Suppose there were only you, Margery, and that I loved you more . . . more than . . . ?"

"Wild honey?" she finished, half crying and half laughing.

"Yes, more than that. My life hasn't been as happy as I tried to tell you on that night. But there's nothing else that I could do. I'm a marked and branded man. The law would never let me rest."

"It wouldn't. It wouldn't," said the girl, and she leaned toward him with a transformed face. "Don't you see? If you went away . . . oh, off to Italy, say, and spent a year or so there . . . who'd ever know you there? In a few years everyone would forget you over here. You'd be as safe as sin in New York, say, after that."

She laughed again. Ching watched the wavering of the light up and down her throat during that laughter, and the growth and the dying of her smile until his hands stretched themselves out to her.

"You have a heart of gold!" Ching burst out. "There is no other woman in the world like you."

"What are you saying now?" she asked in a whisper. "What do you mean by that? You were making a fantastic joke, then, when you talked about the Chinese girl?"

"I was only trying to find an easy way to tell you how I loved you, Margery."

"Did you doubt me?" cried the girl. "Oh, my dear, since that first night I've been ready to follow you around the world. Without a question. Dad knows . . . I've told him . . . he doesn't care . . . he'll fix everything . . . he wants me to marry you . . . he . . . he's ready to make life heaven for us both, Harry. . . ."

"Ah," said Ching, "you would speak like that, as free as the wind of heaven."

He stepped back a little more from her until the full shaft of the moon smote his face.

"If you care for me," he pleaded, "will you care for my friend? I have a friend with me, Margery, who would not dare to love anything but the Chinese girl of whom I spoke to you. You only know Harry Delancey, but now you have a right to know his closest companion."

He fumbled at his head an instant, and then stood before her with the wig in his hand. She saw the high, shaven forehead of a Chinaman, the long gleam of the queue that slid down his back—the very eyes of this man had altered upon the instant, and out of their darkness looked misery and the patient endurance of doom that only the Orient can produce.

Margery slipped back against the wall, and she shut out the new face with both hands clutching across her eyes.

She heard the voice speaking to her. The very voice had altered subtly, now, falling from the clear, crisp tones of Delancey into the soft singsong of the Chinaman.

"I am Harry Delancey," he said, "when I ride the stallion, and wear the gay clothes, and speak English, and rob on the highway. But that man is a lie, and the true man is this Ching Wo . . . who kneels here before you, who kisses the edge of your gown . . . who rises again . . . who sees that he, too, will love you forever . . . who begs you to forgive him and to keep his secret . . . and so he bids you farewell."

Margery snatched the hands from her face. The door had closed. Only the flowers were upon the bed and the moon upon the flowers. She whispered: "Harry . . . Ching Wo . . . I don't care. I want you."

This she said, or tried to say, but grief and fear of losing him had choked her.

So she sprang from the bed and hurried to the door. It moaned beneath her hand as she opened it, but she saw only the empty hall, and, when she leaned over the stairs, they were empty, also.

All she saw was a horseman disappearing down the street, with the moon gleaming like silver on his horse.

At the very moment when the sun rolled up from the east, there came a furtive tap at Margery's door, and she listened with a wild rising of the heart. She crossed the floor on tiptoe and drew the door suddenly open.

Before her was not what she had half dreaded and half hoped to find there, but a small man, slender, roughly clothed, with bright, intelligent eyes fixed upon her face.

He drew off his hat, bowing a little as he did so.

"My name is John Glendon," he said. "I want to speak with you for a moment. I want to show you a letter written to me by a mutual friend. I've ridden half the night to get here with it."

"A mutual friend?" she asked.

"Delancey," he said. "Li Wo raised him to be Chinese, but I taught him the ways of white men, so he could be Harry Delancey. He's no more a Chinaman than I am."

Margery stepped back and waved him into the room. Then, as he entered, she closed the door and stood with her shoulders and head leaning against it, her hand gathering her dressing gown at her throat.

Mr. Glendon took out the letter at once. The stiff paper *crackled* as he unfolded it. Outside, the noise of the reawakening town began, making the night and all that had been in it seem suddenly short and unreal as a dream.

For life was beginning again, wearily, as it had started for human beings 10,000,000 times before, leading once more in the day's course to hope, labor, futility, non-accomplishment, weariness, hope, and sleep again.

He presented the sheet to her and she read:

My Dear Friend;

This is good bye. A thousand times I have wished to tell you what I am going to tell you now, but I never have had the courage until this moment.

I am leaving my old life and I never shall return to it again. I mean, I am leaving my life as Harry Delancey, the white man, and stepping back into the character of Ching Wo, my true self. I am about to start on the trail of Captain Malcolm Foster, and I never shall leave it until I have found him. This time one of us will die, and, unless he has a strong guard and good luck, he will be the dead man and not I!

However, it's not this alone that determines me to become what I truly am—a Chinaman. There is also something more. I've told you a little about Margery Linton. You've guessed a great deal more than I've told. I'm convinced that if I could actually be what I pretend to her that I am—a white man—I could win her. But I can't lie to her to that extent.

I am going to tell her the truth before I step out of the person of Harry Delancey forever. Then I shall have said good bye to the two people who mean the most to me.

I feel for you, my old teacher—you who have coached me in the ways of the white man—not only a great deal of affection and respect, but also a little resentment. I feel that you should have known that it is not right to make a man two things, for the East and the West cannot mix. The result is that my life has become miserable and will never be happy again. However, you have done only what my father wished you to do.

You have given up all the world. But still I should like to have you see Margery Linton. She is noble, gentle, and beautiful. Go to look at her, even if it is only from a distance.

Good bye again,
Ching Wo

P.S. Foster has just heard I've gotten out of jail, and he's started south, probably for the Weyburn Hills. If you want to cut in across that trail, it's likely that you and I may meet and ride together for a few miles.

XXXV

It was not quite dawn when Ching Wo rode out into the forest and went back to the spot where he had left his cache. He opened it and sorted from it all that pertained to the life of the white man.

There were gay clothes, and sashes, and scarves, and more than one jewel, and flaunting hats, and magnificent boots, and silver braids and decorations, and tight-fitting Mexican jackets, and all that the gay heart of youth could desire.

He separated the jewels from this heap, then he touched a match to the remainder. It flared up, and soon was burning fiercely.

Then he stripped off the very clothes he was wearing and cast them upon the fire. Last of all, he dressed himself in cheap, loose garments, such as a Chinese laborer might have worn. He rubbed yellow stain on face and hands and put a cheap felt hat upon his head.

By the time he had accomplished this, the fire had sunk to a scattered glow, so he left that place and went to the edge of the woods, where he faced the gathering pink of the east. Then he mounted his horse and rode for hours.

It was late afternoon, and in the Weyburn Hills the heat of the sun had put the wind to sleep, except for hot, vagrant puffs that raised the dust and let it hang in pale drifts across the trees. Here, where the trail forked beyond a runlet of water that bubbled across its way, Ching paused to let El Rey have a drink.

Then he stepped the stallion across the little stream and regarded the fork of the trail with an anxious eye.

He did not need to wait long, for from the brush at the right out stepped a Chinese laborer in baggy, wrinkled, dusty clothes, and he waved to the left hand path.

Ching, with a nod, loosed the rein of El Rey and went up the trail like a streak. The way dipped up and down over two small ridges, and, coming to a broad plateau beyond, he could see the dust hanging in thin puffs in the stirless air, as if thrown up not long before by the cup-like hoofs of running horses.

Something glided rapidly through the brush and out came the form of Li Wo, riding a tall bay mule, looking half Chinaman and half Mexican, with a broad sombrero on his head. He waved to Ching with a thin-lipped smile of vicious pleasure.

"Foster is not a mile away, and his horse is dying

beneath him," Li Wo announced. "He has become separated from his two comrades."

El Rey started under the impatient heel of the boy, and they swept forward, Ching gritting his teeth, for he knew that the older man had come to see the slaying of Captain Foster. Such grisly curiosity irritated him almost beyond endurance.

So he rode rapidly, dropping Li Wo behind him. Yet still the older man clung to the trail from a safe distance, for the mule was fresh, and strode almost as fast as a galloping horse.

Soon the boy overtook Foster, whose beard was divided by the wind of his gallop. Ching twitched El Rey to the side, into a thick screen of tall brush from behind which he saw Foster rush up, and then rein in his horse and look around, bewildered.

Ching slipped his stallion into the open. Soundlessly he stepped, as one who could move like a wildcat through the wilderness, and with leveled Colt, the youth said calmly: "Behind you, Captain Foster."

The captain jerked himself halfway round with an oath. Then, realizing what had happened, he sat fixed in the saddle, his body shaken by the heavy panting of his horse.

"A little more, Captain Foster," said Ching. "Turn a little more. You haven't a helpless man triced up in the mizzen rigging now . . . you haven't a whip in your hand, but you have a gun. Are you afraid to face me, my friend?"

The captain, pulling at the reins, slowly brought his

horse about until he faced the boy, and started at the sight of the rude, Chinese garb, the battered hat, the keen young face beneath it.

"Delancey!" he exclaimed. "What have you turned into?"

"I have turned into the son of Li Wo, the Chinaman," said the boy.

"Li Wo again!"

"You remember him, Captain Foster? You remember the flogging, and the storm, and the dead Chinese girl who was my mother? You have white skin. I tell you there are dogs with white hides, also. Do you hear me, white dog? There is a gun in your holster. Fill your hand, because *the time has come for one of us!*"

Captain Foster looked at him with an oddly meditative eye. Well he knew that Ching's nervous speed would beat him to the draw, and the accuracy of that uncanny fighter would kill him if it came to such weapons.

"Your own gun is in your hand," he remarked dryly.

"It's now in the holster."

"Then let it stay there!" exclaimed the captain.

Thrusting both spurs deep into his horse's flanks, he hurled the animal straight at his enemy.

It was a well considered and a swift move, but not swift enough to forestall Ching. He whipped up his Colt and covered his man—and then the contorted face—Ching tossed his weapon aside.

What was the satisfaction in a bullet driven accurately home? But a battle hand to hand, such as this big man seemed to desire was still more to his heart. He threw the Colt away. The next moment he was caught in Foster's encircling arms and borne from his horse, while Foster himself, overbalanced, lost his own saddle. They fell with a *crash* into a shrub that ripped long, jagged holes in their clothing, and whipped their flesh with thorns.

Ching dipped his head beneath a threatened blow and whirled his whole body up and away from the other. The captain lurched after him, wonderfully swift in spite of his years and his bulk.

But now the game was played in another fashion. At close grips Foster possessed some chance, but once Ching was free, the big sailor might as well have attacked a will-o'-the-wisp.

His rush struck thin air. He wheeled, planting his heel to stop himself short, and smote with all his might. A bending of the boy's body made that stroke fail. And the next instant he had caught the shooting arm over his shoulder and stooped, swaying all his weight forward.

The captain involuntarily completed his rush against the solid round of a tree trunk. Head and body smote it, so that he reeled heavily back.

His arms were down; his head swayed helplessly from side to side, but his face was still valiantly set for the battle.

The wise and cruel hands of Ching Wo reached for the grip that would be the last of this battle. Yet even then he hesitated, half unwilling. A grim man the skipper might be, but a brave man beyond doubt, and one who asked no quarter.

In spite of himself, Ching could not fix his thumbs in the captain's throat. One moment would end the battle, but although all his memories called out for him to destroy this persecutor of his father, this slayer of his mother, yet murder was not in Ching's heart.

He rose from the fallen man and stood above him, arms akimbo, while a hoarse voice yelled behind him: "Ching, Ching! Now he lies in the hollow of your hand. Now is the time!"

He looked back and saw Li Wo, who had dismounted from the mule and was running toward him, stumbling in haste.

"Or else step back! I can deal with him. By all the bright faces of my ancestors, who watch us now, this is my hour with him, Ching Wo! Oh, my brave lad! Oh, comfort of my life!"

"Comfort yourself in another way, Li Wo," said a dry voice close to them. "You'll never have the life of this man, Li, in spite of all the devils that you think are working for you."

Li Wo checked his infuriated rush. Ching turned, also, and saw John Glendon dismounting from his foam-covered horse. When his foot struck the ground, his knee sagged with weariness, but his eyes were as calm and bright as ever, when he faced them.

"Ching," he said, "or whatever your real name may be . . . Samuel, or John, or Harry, or William . . . keep that yellow-skinned reptile away from your father. Because, as sure as God is in heaven, you are Foster's son!"

236

XXXVI

Now it seemed to Ching that he had been roused suddenly from heavy sleep. The sting of his wounds departed from him. He looked idly up to where a buzzard hung circling in the sky.

Then the form on the ground stirred. Ching looked blankly down at Captain Foster as the latter pushed himself up to a sitting posture.

"If you doubt me," said Glendon, "look at that rat . . . that sneaking, kidnapping, lying Chinaman."

Li Wo's nerve strength, which had sustained him through many a crisis, faded in this one. For he remembered with bitter vividness the ropes that had gripped him on the mizzen rigging of the clipper. Once more he seemed to hear the whip *hiss* in the air, and feel the cut of its lashes.

He turned in a sudden panic to flee, and found Glendon and a steady gun before him. Li Wo turned pale.

Then the voice of big Malcolm Foster sounded heavily.

"Son?" he cried. "Son to whom?"

"Li Wo will tell you," said Glendon in the same acid tones. "Li, speak up. Here are several angry men. Here is a rope, also, and trees with very strong branches. You understand me? But an ounce of truth at this moment, Li, may prove a pound of cure for you and your . . . neck."

Li Wo stared at Glendon with a tigerish rage, and then his quick eye went from face to face—to big Malcolm Foster, half staggering still, but suspended with interest and bewilderment—to the boy, last of all, he who had been a treasure trove that Li had so thoroughly exploited.

And as he glanced at Ching, at the anger and doubt that were beginning to rise in that young face, the strength to resist passed suddenly from Li Wo.

"It is true, then," he confessed. "That man used a whip to scourge a Chinaman. I took his own son and made him a whip on the backs of the whites. The boy who I have called Ching is your son, not mine."

He pointed at Malcolm Foster with a trembling forefinger, then turned and fled to his mule.

The captain, who only gradually had come to realize what Li Wo's words meant, now boomed out such a terrible note that Li Wo gave a shrill cry like a rabbit in a hound's jaws. But he was already in the saddle and, bending far forward, flogged the mule into a hasty gallop. That was the last young Foster ever saw of his Chinese "father", although long afterward a rumor reached him from the Sierras that Li Wo was bossing a gang of coolies in the construction of the great Central Pacific Railroad.

Captain Foster turned slowly toward the boy. Their glances met without hostility but with amazement as they threw off the rage of battle that had been burning in them, and gradually found in each other that thing for which each had the most profound desire in this world.

Glendon, recognizing the sanctity of the moment, stepped quietly out of the picture and rode away.

For some time father and son stood without a word—then followed eager questions and explanations. They watched the dying of the day and the gradual growth of moonlight that still left the valley unillumined but touched the polished rock faces and white birch bark with ghostly radiance.

Then said the son: "Now, if you don't mind, I'll ride over to Linton's claim. You see, I have a tryst to keep. Good bye for a little while."

And leaping on the back of El Rey, the boy was gone. Captain Foster narrowed his eyes as he watched with pride the form of a rider on a silver steed drifting among the shadows, indistinct as an old memory, subtle as perfume that filled the air with a scent of wild honey.

Center Point Publishing
600 Brooks Road ● PO Box 1
Thorndike ME 04986-0001 USA

(207) 568-3717

US & Canada:
1 800 929-9108
www.centerpointlargeprint.com